or things are purely coincidental. Names, characters, places and events are products of this author's imagination.

DEDICATION

To my granddaughter, Leah, who loves to read about mysteries, adventures and everything that is creative

ABBY & HOLLY SERIES BOOK 2

Unfortunate Events

JANICE SPINA

Cover & Illustrations by

John Spina

Copyright 2018
By Janice Spina

Published by Janice Spina 2018

Library of Congress Control Number: 2018912285

This book is a work of fiction. Any references to persons, places

ACKNOWLEDGEMENTS

Thank you to my beta readers, Patricia Bradley, Michelle Clement James, Michele Rolfe, and John Spina, for their tireless efforts to read and review this book and for their helpful input. Their assistance is invaluable and appreciated.

A special thank you to my husband, John, for the lovely chapter illustrations and the beautiful cover of this book.

OTHER BOOKS BY JANICE SPINA:

Pre-School to Grade Three:

Louey the Lazy Elephant

Ricky the Rambunctious Raccoon

Jerry the Crabby Crayfish
(Pinnacle Book Achievement Award)

Lamby the Lonely Lamb
(Silver Medal from Mom's Choice Awards)

Jesse the Precocious Polar Bear

Broose the Moose on the Loose
(Pinnacle Book Achievement Award)

Sebastian Meets Marvin the Monkey

Colby the Courageous Cat
(Pinnacle Book Achievement Award)

Jeffrey the Jittery Giraffe
(Pinnacle Book Achievement Award)

Clarence Henry the Hermit Crab

Lucy the Talented Toy Terrier

Middle-Grade/Preteen/YA:

The Case of the Missing Cell Phone

(Davey & Derek Junior Detectives Series, Book 1)

(Pinnacle Book Achievement Award & Reader's Favorite Book Awards – Honorable Mention)

The Case of the Mysterious Black Cat

(Davey & Derek Junior Detectives Series, Book 2)

(Pinnacle Book Achievement Award)

The Case of the Magical Ivory Elephant

(Davey & Derek Junior Detectives Series, Book 3)

(Pinnacle Book Achievement Award & Silver Medal from Reader's Favorite Book Awards)

The Case of the Brown Scraggly Dog

(Davey & Derek Junior Detectives Series, Book 4)

The Case of the Sad Mischievous Ghost

(Davey & Derek Junior Detectives Series, Book 5)

(Pinnacle Book Achievement Award & Silver Medal from Authorsdb Cover Contest)

Abby & Holly Series Book 1, School Dance

<u>Novels: (under J.E. Spina)</u>

Hunting Mariah

(Finalist in Authorsdb First Lines
Contest)

How Far Is Heaven

An Angel Among Us (A Short Story Collection)

Mariah's Revenge (Sequel to Hunting Mariah)

Table of Contents

INTRODUCTION

This is **Book 2** of the **Abby & Holly Series**. This Series is a spin-off from **Davey & Derek Junior Detective Series, Book 5, The Case of the Sad Mischievous Ghost.**

Abby and Holly, first cousins on their mothers' side, appeared in **Book 5** of the **Davey & Derek Series** when they enlisted the twins' help to capture some ghosts that inhabited Abby Rizzo's house.

There is still one ghost that has returned to haunt their house. Her name is Felicity. She has become the protector of Abby and Holly and refuses to leave until she feels that the cousins don't need her anymore.

Holly Lester is living with Abby and her family until Holly's parents return from a business trip overseas. When they return, Holly's parents will have to find a home of their own or live with the Rizzo's until they do.

Abby has long brown hair and green eyes. She wants to be a fashion designer one day. Holly has long blonde tresses and blue eyes. She wants to be an author and write all kinds of mysteries.

Now the girls are in their own series doing what girls like to do. They have their own adventures, solve mysteries, and interact with the twins,

Davey and Derek Donato, from time to time.

This book touches on handling unexpected incidents and how to overcome disappointments in life.

These middle-grade books carry life lessons that encourage children, preteens and young adults to be kind, caring and sensitive to others' feelings. The characters show respect toward one another and are polite to their parents and others. I will never have any offensive language or subject matter in these stories.

Watch for book 3 coming in 2019 with a new adventure for the girls and book 6 of Davey & Derek Series also coming in 2019 with a new case for the twins to solve.

CHAPTER ONE

Welcome Visitors

Holly raced back and forth making sure everything was in order. She thoroughly cleaned her side of the bedroom she shared with her cousin while Abby cleaned hers.

Abby could feel the excitement emitted by Holly. She knew that this was a nerve-wracking time for her cousin as Holly's parents were expected within the hour. They had been away for six months treating patients in third world countries. Holly's father is a doctor while her mother is a nurse.

"Holly, slow down. You're going to wear yourself out. Don't worry, everything is perfect. Your parents aren't going to notice the house, all they'll see is you."

"Yeah, I guess, Abby. But I have to do something. I am shaking all over with nerves. I know I'm going to break down when I see them."

"Of course you will. Look, I have two boxes of tissues, one for you and the other for your mother. I won't charge a penny for any used," Abby chuckled.

Holly smiled and nodded as she continued to fold and tuck and flutter around their room looking for something to fix.

Abby sighed and reached out to Holly, "Listen, why don't we go downstairs and have a snack. Mom has plenty of stuff prepared for your parents when they arrive. She won't notice if we take a few."

Grabbing Holly by the arm, Abby tugged and pulled her out of their room and headed downstairs to the kitchen. Jane Rizzo, Abby's mother, was busy preparing more food for their dinner later that evening.

"Hi girls. What do you need? Want a snack? I have plenty of everything in the fridge. Help yourselves."

Abby winked at Holly and said, "See I told you!"

"Sure, Aunt Jane. Thanks." Holly rolled her eyes and laughed, feeling a little less anxious.

The girls snacked on some chips and spinach dip and were putting away their plates as the doorbell rang.

Bob Rizzo called out, "I'll get it."

Holly and Abby ran to the front door as the door was being opened by Abby's father. Standing in the doorway looking tired and bedraggled after a long flight were Holly's parents, Jay and Shirley Lester.

"Mom, Dad!" Holly jumped into their open arms and buried her head in her mother's neck as she cried.

"Oh, honey, I've missed you so much. How are you? You look so grown up. My God, you are growing up to be a young woman now. Jay, look at our girl! She's beautiful!"

"Yes, she is," Jay agreed. Turning to Holly, "I've missed you, sweetie. You have grown since we last saw you. It's been a long time. We need to catch up." Hugs and kisses were shared as they came into the house.

Shirley backed up to look her daughter over from head to toe. Holly sniffled and blew her nose and continued to pull more tissues from the box Abby held out to her.

Jane stepped forward and hugged her sister and brother-in-law and welcomed them into the house. Bob kissed his sister-in-law's cheek and gave Jay's hand a hardy shake.

"Come in and sit down. Bob will take your suitcases and put them into your room upstairs. We have the third floor all ready for you."

After everyone was settled in the living room, Jane went to get the refreshments. She wiped the tears that were falling as she went to the kitchen.

Bob came back after dropping off the suitcases and stopped by the kitchen to give his wife a hand. When he noticed Jane's tears Bob wrapped his arms around her and gave her a tight squeeze.

"Hey, honey. You okay?"

"Now I am, Bob. Thank you, sweetheart. You always know what to do when I feel emotional."

"That's my job, honey," Bob smiled and picked up the plate of hors d'oeuvres and carried them into the living room for their guests.

Jane followed closely behind with the drinks on a tray. She could hear the excited chatter of her sister and niece as they began to catch up on the past six months.

"Mom, we had a ton of fun at the dance. I'll have to show you our dresses. They're beautiful!"

"Oh my goodness, I can't wait to see them. You'll have to model them for me. Okay?"

Exchanging delighted looks, the girls nodded in unison. "Yes, we would love to dress up again and show them off."

Jane added, "They looked gorgeous, Shirley. Their dates were handsome too. Let me get the photos. I made copies for you."

"Thanks, Sis. You are the best. I can't thank you enough for all you have done for us by taking care of Holly," Shirley chocked up and had to stop.

"It's okay, Shirl. It's all fine. Holly has done well here and in school. She's a good kid too and no problem at all. She's like my second daughter." Jane squeezed Holly's shoulder and bent over to kiss her sister's tear-stained cheek before going to look for the photos to share with her.

Jane placed the photos on her sister's lap. She made up a plate for Shirley, who looked too tired to reach forward and do that herself. Jane placed both the plate and a cold glass of iced tea in front of her sister.

"Thank you, Jane. I'll treasure these photos." Shirley sighed and continued, "We're awfully tired. Do you think we could lay down for a little while after we finish our drinks and snacks?"

"I don't see why not. The room is ready for you.

Jay nodded in agreement, "Yes, I think we could both use a little nap to refresh us and maybe a quick shower when we wake up. We'll feel like new."

"I do feel sticky and uncomfortable from the long flight. You don't mind, sweetheart, do you? We can catch up some more after I wake up and shower."

"It's okay, Mom. I understand. How long was your flight?"

"Oh, about 9-10 hours total and we changed planes twice."

"Oh boy, I don't think I wouldn't like being on a plane that long. In fact,

I've never been on a plane," Holly announced.

"Well sweetie, one day we'll all go somewhere on a plane for a vacation."

"Really, Mom? I can't wait!" Holly's face lit up and the anxiety that marked it earlier dissipated.

Shirley and Jay finished up their drinks and hors d'oeuvres and stood.

"Bob will take you up to your room, Sis. It can get a little confusing. We have a lot of rooms upstairs. Three more bedrooms and a few bathrooms. We only updated yours and an adjoining bathroom. The rest is not habitable right now. We really don't need them at the moment. Maybe in the future we could make a complete apartment up there for someone." Jane stopped talking when she noticed her sister's eyes beginning to close. "Never mind, we can talk about that later. Get some rest."

Bob led the way for the tired couple and opened up the door to their bedroom.

"Wow, this is lovely, Bob. Thank you and Jane so much for doing this. You must have spent a fortune redoing this room and bathroom. It's just perfect after what we have been living in the past six months. This is a real luxury and deeply appreciated."

"No problem at all, Shirley and Jay. You are family and we do what we can for family. Now rest and we'll see you when you feel like coming down. Dinner will be around 6:00 if you are able. See you later.

CHAPTER TWO

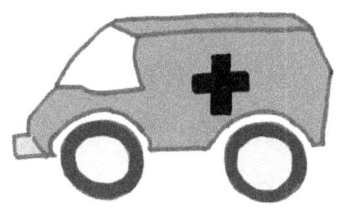

Health Issues

Jane and Bob cleared up the plates, glasses, leftovers and returned to the kitchen. They wanted to discuss things without the girls hearing.

"I'm worried about Shirley. She doesn't look well. I bet she's not taking care of herself. She is a diabetic, you know. I hope she's taking her shots."

"Jane, you worry too much. Relax and enjoy your sister's visit. You can talk to her about it later and allay your fears. She is a nurse and knows how to take care of sick people especially herself."

"Well, maybe you're right, Bob. But I'm the oldest even if it is only by two years and I always took care of her. I can't stop now."

"Ok honey, whatever makes you feel better. Give her some space though, okay?"

"Of course, dear."

Bob rolled his eyes and left the room to do some work on the computer.

Jane went back to thinking about what she would say to her sister about her health and about not going back to work in foreign countries.

She wanted her sister to stay with her, Bob and the girls. She planned on fixing up the third floor into a beautiful apartment for Shirley, Jay and Holly.

Jane knew her sister was stubborn, but so was she. She needed to convince Shirley that this was the right thing to do, for Holly most of all.

***

"I'm so happy to have my parents back, Abby. They both look thin though, don't you think? My mom looks a little pale and sickly. I hope it's just the long flight. Maybe she'll perk up after she has some rest and a good meal."

"Sure, that will do it, Holly. Don't worry, okay? They're both fine. They know about medicine, being a doctor and nurse. If they were sick they would treat themselves. Wouldn't they?"

"I guess, Abby. But I'm still worried. You remember Justine and how sick she got not eating correctly."

"Yeah, I remember." Abby thought back to the time that their friend Justine got sick from eating too much sugar which was snuck into her pudding at school by the two girls who bullied her. That was scary for not only Justine but for her and Holly too. She kept quiet and didn't say any more to upset her cousin.

"Hey Holly, let's take out our dresses so you can show your mother when she wakes up. We can fix up our hair with some curls, put on some lip gloss and dress up as if we were going to the dance."

"That's a great idea, Abby! I love it! Mom will too!"

The girls kept busy for an hour or so fixing up their hair and nails, applying lip gloss and prancing around in their dresses.

Jane went up to the girls' room with their newly washed clothes for them to fold. She stopped in the doorway and gasped. There stood the girls all decked out like they were going to the dance again.

"Wow, you look beautiful once again, girls!"

"Oh, hi Mom, didn't see you there. We dressed up for Aunt Shirley."

"Oh, that's nice. I'm sure she will love to see you both all dressed up. She hasn't come down yet though. I'll leave your clothes on the bed. Fold them when you can and bring the basket back to the laundry room. Thanks, girls."

"Okay, Mom."

Jane went up another flight to her sister's room. She listened outside the door but there was no sound. She didn't want to disturb them by knocking. She would have to wait until they came down on their own accord. In the meantime, she would start dinner. She was preparing a roast beef with potatoes, peas and carrots, gravy, and a tossed salad. She had baked an apple pie the day before. She wanted everything to be perfect for her sister.

Jay woke up next to his wife and gently touched her arm. She didn't respond. He felt her forehead and grabbed his BP cuff to take her blood pressure. It registered lower than usual for her. He next pulled out her blood sugar kit and noted her sugar was low also. He ran downstairs taking two stairs at a time to get help.

Jane looked out from the kitchen when Jay came into the room out of breath.

"What's wrong, Jay?"

"It's Shirley. I need to get her to drink some orange juice right away. Her BP is low and so is her sugar. The trip did a job on her, and I don't think she gave herself the second shot of insulin."

"No problem, Jay. Here's some OJ. Let me know what else I can do. I know she's in good hands with you."

The girls heard someone taking the stairs in a hurry and stuck their heads out to see Holly's dad race by.

"Dad, what's wrong? Where's Mom?"

"She's still resting, honey. I'll be right back. I'm getting her a drink. She woke up thirsty."

"Oh, okay, Dad. Tell Mom to come down to our room to see us. We dressed up for her."

"Okay, honey, maybe in a little while. She needs to rest some more."

"Oh, okay. Are you sure she's okay?"

"Umm, yes, she's fine, Holly. You look beautiful by the way."

"Thanks, Dad."

Abby and Holly exchanged worried looks. "What if something is wrong with my mother, Abby?"

"Don't worry, Holly. Your dad is a doctor. He knows what to do. He can take care of anything wrong. He did say she woke up thirsty and just needs more rest."

"Yeah, but he doesn't always tell me the truth about Mom. He doesn't want me to worry. He knows that I always worry about losing her. My grandmother on my father's side died of complications from diabetes when I was just a baby. I'm afraid that could happen to my mother too."

"Oh, I didn't know your paternal grandmother had diabetes. That means you have it on both sides of your family. You need to be careful, Holly."

"Yeah, I know. I am bound to get it too," Holly sighed.

"Well, that means you are susceptible, but doesn't mean you will get it for sure." Abby backed away from the mirror to look at her cousin who was now crying.

"Oh, I'm sorry for saying anything at all, Holly. You'll be fine. You're healthy, young and strong."

As Abby was consoling her cousin, Jay ran by their room again. The girls followed him downstairs to see what was going on.

Jane and Bob met him at the bottom of the stairs with a phone in hand. He took it and dialed 911 for an ambulance. Shirley was sicker than just needing some sugar. She was in a diabetic coma.

They all waited at the front door for the ambulance and directed the EMTs to the third floor. Jay rode along in the ambulance with his wife and said he would call when she was stable.

Jane and Bob called out, "Girls, change quickly. We'll be in the car waiting for you. We're all going to the hospital to wait for word on how your mother is doing. I can't wait around here."

The girls went back upstairs and changed. Jane shut the oven off and took the roast out and covered it along with the rest of the vegetables. She hoped it would not spoil. It could be a long night at the hospital.

CHAPTER THREE

Good News

"Aunt Jane, will Mom be okay?"

"Oh honey, of course, she will be as soon as they get her sugar under control. Evidently she forgot to take her insulin last night before she got on the plane. Don't worry, honey. Okay? She has your dad overseeing everything too. He won't let anything happen to her." Jane said a silent prayer that she was right for her niece's sake. She didn't voice her concerns that her sister might not make it.

After an hour and a half Jay came out to talk to them. His face was pale and he was sweating.

"She's going to be okay, everyone. She needs to stay overnight at the least to get her stabilized. After that she'll need to rest at your house. We will have to delay our trip back until she is healthy enough to go."

"Jay, you can't be serious? Shirl can't go back there in her state even if she is stable." Jane's face was scarlet with anger.

"We'll talk later, Jane. I'm going to stay overnight with Shirley. Why don't you all go back home and eat dinner? I'll call you tomorrow about her condition."

Jane couldn't talk and sat still fuming as Bob answered for her, "No problem, Jay. We're relieved that Shirley is better. Talk to you tomorrow. Get some rest yourself tonight. Call me and I'll come and pick you both up when you are ready to leave here."

"Thanks, Bob. Goodnight."

"Dad, can I go see Mom now?"

"No, honey. She's asleep and will be for the night. I'll call you tomorrow and you'll see her then. Don't worry, honey. She'll be fine. Go home with Aunt Jane and Uncle Bob. Okay? I love you."

"I love you too, Dad. Give Mom a kiss for me."

"I will, honey. Goodnight."

Holly sat silently crying in the back seat with Abby holding her hand and feeding her tissues. Holly squeezed her cousin's hand and sighed deeply.

"It's okay, Holly. Your mom will be back with us tomorrow. She needs to stay overnight. It's the best place for her."

"I know, but why couldn't my dad take care of her at your house. He is a doctor."

"He doesn't have all the equipment and medical supplies, Holly."

"What if something happens to my mother, Abby? Is she going to die?" Holly cried harder and wiped copious tears with more tissues.

Jane listened from the front seat and turned toward Holly. "Your mom is going to be okay. You heard your father. He's staying there with her to make sure she's doing well overnight. She needs to rest and get her strength back and her sugar to a safe level. She'll be back with us tomorrow. You wait and see. Then you can catch up some more with her. Okay, honey?"

Holly sniffled and gulped back tears. "Okay, Aunt Jane."

Abby kept her cousin's hand tightly gripped in hers and bumped shoulders with Holly to make her stop crying. It worked for a few minutes but Holly began crying again when she thought about not being able to show her mother her dress and share more about what transpired over the past six months. What if she dies? Then she would be without a mother. What would she do?

Once back at the house Jane checked over the dinner and returned it to the oven. It was not quite cooked yet. She didn't know if anyone was hungry now, but she would try her best to see that they did eat.

Bob set the table and pulled out a bottle of wine for himself and Jane to sip as they waited for dinner to be ready. The girls went up to their room until they were called down to dinner.

Holly washed her face and lay down on the bed. She had a terrible headache and her stomach felt queasy. She didn't want to eat anything. The smell of the roast was making her sicker.

She closed her eyes to rest and the next thing she saw was Felicity. The ghost was hovering over Holly as she slept. She was sitting up even though her body was still prone.

Holly heard Felicity's voice in her head.

Don't worry, my friend.

This is not the end.

Your mother will recover.

She will soon be home over you to hover.

Eat well and stay strong.

And nothing else will go wrong.

Holly jumped up suddenly and looked around the room. There was no sign of Felicity or her cousin.

"Abby, where are you?"

Abby came out of the bathroom in a hurry when she heard the urgency in her cousin's voice.

"What's wrong, Holly? Are you okay?"

"Yeah, I'm fine now. I dreamt of Felicity. She told me my mother is going to be okay and that I should eat and get strong so nothing will go wrong."

"Really, you saw her again? I wish I could see her too. Let's go down for dinner. I'm starving. It smells delicious. Mom made apple pie for dessert too! Yummy! She makes the best!"

Felicity listened and smiled. She was planning on a surprise for Abby later that night.

Dinner was a success even though everyone was concerned for Shirley. Their hunger took over and they cleaned their plates and waited for pie. That, too, was enjoyed.

Jane put away the leftovers in case Shirley and Jay were hungry when they came home the next day. She was also planning on another special dinner just to celebrate her homecoming once again. This time, hopefully for good.

***

Later that night after Holly and Abby were all talked out and fast asleep, Felicity visited the girls once again. This time she hovered over Abby's sleeping body and waited to talk to her.

Abby looked up in her dream when she saw Felicity. She was surprised and happy at the same time that Felicity visited her for a change.

Abby, my friend, take care of Holly.

She needs you most of all, no folly.

Her mother will soon be home.

But her father will want to roam.

Abby nodded in her sleep and Felicity disappeared into midair.

The next morning Abby couldn't wait for Holly to wake up so she could tell her about her dream of Felicity.

"Holly, are you awake yet?"

"Huh, what did you say, Abby?"

"I have to tell you about my dream. I saw Felicity in my dream. She was so real. I couldn't believe it! She came to me this time! I'm so excited!"

"That's great, Abby. What did she say to you?"

"She said that I need to take care of you. Your mother would be home soon, but your father will want to go away again."

"Oh, I was afraid of that. I know Dad feels like he has to help people everywhere. He is a kind and caring man, but he should be taking care of Mom instead of others. Is that all she said?"

"Yes, but I felt that she wanted to say more but stopped herself. Maybe Felicity will visit us in our dreams again and tell us more."

"Yeah, maybe she will," Holly mused. Under her breath she said, "I hope she does."

CHAPTER FOUR

Catching Up Again

Bob got off the phone and grabbed his keys. "Hey, honey, that was Jay. They're ready to come home. You stay here and prepare breakfast or lunch. We'll be right back."

"Okay, honey. Thanks. I'll let the girls know. Holly will be relieved."

Jane slowly walked up to the girls' room and stopped at the top of the stairs when she overheard them talking.

"That's wonderful that Felicity appeared to you, Abby. She's a friend to both of us after all."

"Yeah, I guess. But I was thinking that she liked you better."

"Well, maybe I can keep secrets better than you can," Holly giggled.

"No you can't. You told me everything that Felicity said to you, didn't you?"

Jane walked in before Holly could answer. "Hi girls. Dad went to get Shirley and Jay at the hospital. He'll be back shortly. Why don't you come down and have a late breakfast or brunch. I am fixing plenty to eat. It's too early for lunch but not too late for breakfast, so we'll have brunch."

"Sounds great, Mom. Pancakes, sausages and everything?"

"Yes, and everything. Come down and give me a hand. You girls can set the table for me and help flip the pancakes. What were you talking about just now?"

"Oh nothing much," Abby answered, locking eyes with Holly.

"Who's Felicity?"

"Oh, she's the ghost that inhabited our house. Remember Davey and Derek exorcised her and two other ghosts from the house?"

"Oh yes, so you told us. I never did see them though."

"That's right. You didn't. Maybe you weren't supposed to see them, only all of us kids."

"Yeah, maybe. But you didn't answer my question. Why were you talking about Felicity now? Did she come back?" Jane followed the girls downstairs but never did get an answer to her question before the door opened and in walked Bob with Shirley and Jay.

"Mom, I'm so glad you're home again. Are you feeling better now?"

"Hi sweetheart. I'm fine. Just needed a good rest. Even though in the hospital they woke me up every few hours to check my sugar," Shirley sighed still looking pale and tired.

"That's to be expected, Shirl. They needed to know that your sugar was returning to normal. Next time I will give you a shot. We rushed to get on the plane and both forgot about the time change. I'll have to keep a closer watch on you, honey."

Shirley smiled, but didn't respond to Jay. She held onto her daughter and was led to a comfortable chair in the living room.

"Hi Sis. Are you hungry? I made a brunch. Wasn't sure if you had a good breakfast so I combined a little of both for you in case."

"Hmm, I could eat one of your famous pancakes if you made them."

"Oh, I knew you liked them, and yes, I have plenty for everyone. Come into the dining room and sit. I will serve you some. You need to build up your strength. I have sugar substitute for you too. I know you need to watch the carbs and sugars."

"Thanks, Jane. You are the best. One pancake is good and some bacon, eggs, and fruit. I will be stuffed after this. May have to take another nap," Shirley sighed with a smile.

Bob ushered Jay into the dining room and the girls hovered around the table bringing platters of scrambled eggs, bacon, sausages, spinach quiche, hash browns, pancakes, even roast beef sandwiches, and finally, a large fruit bowl.

Jane placed a full pot of coffee on the table for everyone to help themselves along with jugs of water and milk.

The men dug in like they hadn't eaten for a week. Jane and Shirley exchanged chuckles as they watched their husbands eat and chat in between bites.

Bob looked up and smiled at his wife. "Everything is delicious, Jane. Nice job, honey."

"Yes, Jane. It's wonderful. I've been stuffing my mouth so full I couldn't tell you. Thank you. We needed this. Best meal we've had in a long time, huh, Shirl?"

"Oh, it certainly is, Jane. Thank you for everything. You are the best big sister anyone could ever have."

"No problem. I wanted to make your first day here special but that didn't work out last night. At least I could make a hardy meal for you today."

"Well, you outdid yourself, Sis. I'll be full until late tonight."

"Well, you better save some room for tonight's dinner. We're having a cookout. It's a beautiful day. Bob is doing the honors on the grill with steaks and wings. I'll make potato salad and tossed salad."

"Oh, boy, can't wait, Bob. I haven't had a steak in six months. In fact, that was the last meal we had here with you before we left." Jay patted Bob on the back and sighed. He rubbed his full belly and sipped his coffee.

Holly sat next to her mother touching her arm, hand, and hair intermittently. She was relieved to have her home safe and well again. She kept a steady chatter filling her mother in on the past six months.

Shirley smiled and nodded as she listened to her daughter's happy monologue. She wasn't feeling herself yet but hoped to lay down and rest once Holly finished catching her up on all things important.

Abby finished up her food and began to clear up some of the leftovers and empty plates. She wanted to give

Holly some time to spend with her mother alone.

Jane noticed what Abby was doing and joined her at the sink to begin washing dishes and putting food away. She leaned over and kissed her daughter's cheek and said, "You're a good daughter, Abby. Thank you for helping me clean up and for giving your cousin some time with her mother. That's so sweet of you."

"Holly's been upset, Mom. She needs her mother. I wouldn't know what to do without you in my life every day. She only gets to see her mother for two weeks after six months away."

Jane hugged her daughter and agreed. "I know sweetie. It's been tough on Holly. But she is lucky to have such a wonderful cousin who is more like her sister."

"Yep, that's us. We're like sisters. I always tell Holly that. It makes her happy, me too!"

"You two remind me of my sister and me growing up. We were closer than sisters – more like twins. We are only two years apart. We shared everything that girls share, like you and Holly. By the way, what was that about Felicity?"

Shirley came over to her sister and gave her a big hug in thanks. Once again Jane did not get an answer to her question about the ghost.

***

Felicity chuckled as she watched and listened in as Mrs. Rizzo tried to find out about her and failed once again to get an answer from Abby. She would keep careful watch over Holly and her mother. She didn't like the looks, however, of Mrs. Lester's pale face.

CHAPTER FIVE

Keeping Watch

Felicity waited for a chance to talk to the girls that night. She floated around the ceiling in a cloud of flowing hair and a gossamer gown.

The girls were chattering away in the bathroom as they prepared to get ready for bed. Jane came into the girls' room to say good night and felt as if she were being watched. She looked up at the twenty-foot ceiling as the ghost swept by. All she saw was a filmy cloud floating by.

Jane felt a tingle along her arms and on the back of her neck. *What was that? Could that be the ghost, Felicity, the girls have been talking about?*

"Girls, please come out as soon as you are finished brushing your teeth. I need to speak with you."

"Okay, Mom. Be right there."

Abby rinsed her mouth at one of the double sinks and gave her hair one last brush and went out to see what was wrong. She could tell by the tone in her mother's voice that something wasn't right.

Holly came up alongside Abby and they exchanged quizzical looks and shrugged.

Jane was still glancing up at the ceiling as the girls stood in front of her watching. They looked up and studied the high ceiling and sighed.

"What are you looking at, Mom?"

"I thought I saw something up there. It was…I don't know. Maybe it's my imagination, but I thought I saw something wispy like a cloud floating by."

Holly gasped and grabbed hold of Abby's hand and squeezed.

"What did you say, Aunt Jane?"

"Oh, never mind. I don't see it now. It must have been a spider web or something. No worries. I will get a ladder and clean the ceiling in the morning. I came up to say goodnight to you and see how Holly was doing."

"I'm fine, Aunt Jane. I'm happy to have Mom home again."

"Yes, me too. Don't worry about her. I'll watch over her and make sure she's taking her shots and eating properly. She may get sick of me hovering though."

"Thank you, Aunt Jane. You're the best sister and aunt. With you taking care of her I won't worry anymore."

"That's what I wanted – for you not to worry. Okay? Your mom will be fine in no time. She just needs her rest. Let's give her a few days and then we can take in a movie or shopping or go out to lunch, the four of us. Okay?"

"Yes, yes, that would be perfect, Aunt Jane. Thank you."

"Yes, Mom. That would be cool!"

"Okay, girls, jump into bed and get some rest. It's been a hectic couple of days for all of us. Sleep tight my honeys!" The girls giggled and reached up to kiss Jane's cheeks.

"Night Mom! I love you!"

"I love you too!"

"Night, Aunt Jane. I love you lots!"

"I love you both whole bunches!"

More giggles and then the girls settled down and snuggled into their pillows and sighed.

Jane looked up one more time at the ceiling before leaving their room.

"I guess I am a little tired, Abby. How about you?"

"Me too. But what was Mom looking at? Do you think she really saw Felicity?"

"Maybe she did. We never see Felicity when we're awake, only when we're sleeping, in our dreams."

"Hmm, Felicity must have something important to share with us. Maybe we'll see her when we are awake too," Abby mused.

"Yeah, maybe we will. Goodnight."

"Goodnight, Holly."

Felicity floated closer to the girls' bed and settled down next to it. She never sat but drifted a few inches above the floor. She waited to hear their rhythmic breathing then began to talk to them in a singsong manner.

Watch over Shirley.

Watch over her health.

She may not recover early.

Overseas, there is no wealth.

Don't let your father take Shirley.

There is danger ahead - use stealth.

Do what you can to keep them here.

*The way back is filled with danger
that's clear.*

A tiny bell sounded as Felicity ended her warning. It was light and high pitched. Holly opened her eyes to the sound and a second after, so did Abby.

"I heard a bell, Abby. Did you hear it too?"

"Yes, I thought it was my alarm, but I hadn't put it on. I also heard Felicity. She is warning us of some danger ahead."

"I heard her too. I need to warn my mother and father not to fly back. They have to stay here now!"

Abby looked at her alarm clock. "It's only 4:00 am. Too early to wake anyone. We better go back to sleep. Maybe Felicity will tell us more in our sleep."

The girls tossed and turned but could not go to sleep. At least they thought they didn't sleep but Felicity knew better as she heard their breathing level off once again.

Please don't fret.

Please don't forget.

The warning I give.

Is for them to be safe and to live.

A bell sounded once again.

Somewhere across time and space another entity closed off satisfied that the warning was delivered. Mianna, (Davey and Derek's Great Aunt Gigi's cat whose spirit lived in a crystal ball) listened in to Felicity's warning. She kept in touch with Felicity since she saw what was coming. Once Holly's parents arrived Mianna had seen the danger for them if they returned to their jobs as doctor and nurse.

***

Three hours later at 7:00 am the girls woke up and looked around. They listened for the sound of the bell but all was quiet.

"Felicity was here again. She continued with her warning, Holly."

"I know. It sounds creepy that she would know about what could happen. I wonder what she sees. Is it a plane crash or is there some danger in the countries where my parents are scheduled to work?"

"Good question. Maybe she will tell us next time. What was that bell about? We are hearing bells again. Remember the bells we heard when Gigi laughed? It did sound different though, and had only one bell ringing at a time."

"Yes, I agree. This bell was different – higher pitched and only one tinkling sound. Strange though, isn't it?"

"We should ask Felicity about it. Maybe it's like hanging up a phone call. It designates the end."

"Could be, Holly. But we need to tell your parents about this. Do you think they'll believe us?"

"I don't know. My dad probably won't but maybe my mother will. I'll find out soon enough."

CHAPTER SIX

A Dire Announcement

Abby and Holly discussed what they would say to their parents. They had to tell them what Felicity said even if their parents didn't believe it.

By the time the girls went down for breakfast their parents were sitting at the table having coffee and chatting.

The girls chirped up together, "Hi everyone. Good morning."

"Good morning, girls. We didn't want to wake you. I peeked into your room earlier and you were both fast asleep," Jane announced as she began to scramble eggs and fry bacon.

"I guess we were tired and needed our beauty sleep," Abby laughed.

Holly was quiet and smiled as she studied her mother's still pale face.

"How are you feeling today, Mom?"

"I'm doing much better, honey. Slept through the night and feel more rested this morning."

"Thank goodness, Mom. You still look pale though. Maybe you need to get some sun and fresh air. Do you want to go outside for a short walk today?"

"Let's see how I feel in a little while after breakfast. Okay?"

"Sure. Okay." Holly kissed her mother's cheek and sat down to eat next to Abby, who bumped her shoulder and smiled.

"Are you okay, Holly? You're serious and quiet this morning. Did you sleep well?"

"Umm, yeah I'm good, Mom."

Shirley observed her daughter's posture and noticed her smile did not reach her eyes. Something was bothering her.

After breakfast Shirley took her daughter aside and said, "Honey, let's go for a little walk. It would do me good to get some sun and fresh air like you suggested."

"Really, Mom! Great! Let's go."

Shirley nodded at her sister and left the house with her arm tucked into Holly's. It would be good to be away from everyone in order to find out what was bothering her daughter.

They walked a block before either said anything. Holly was rehearsing what she would say to her mother. She was about to explain as Shirley started talking.

"Honey, what's wrong? I can tell there's a problem. Your face says it all. You are always cheerful and smiling. Today you are morose and depressed. Will you share it with me? Two heads are better than one. We can work out whatever it is together."

"Well, it's hard to explain. You may not believe it if I told you. Let me first explain what happened with the ghosts that were in the house when we moved here."

Holly explained about Davey and Derek and how they exorcised the ghosts. She then continued to describe the previous ghostly visits with the ghost named Felicity.

"Did you actually see this ghost? How do you know her name? Did she tell you?"

"Yes to both questions. Recently Felicity has been appearing to both Abby and me during our dreams."

"Really? How interesting. She contacts you while you are sleeping?"

"Yes, it was creepy the first time we saw her. Now we see and hear her talking to us in our sleep."

"What does she say to you?" Shirley asked with a serious and concerned expression on her face.

Holly explained about the girls who were bullying her friend, Justine, and what she did to help them.

"Last night she gave us a warning about you and dad."

"A warning about Dad and me? What kind of warning?"

"Well, she said you shouldn't go back to work overseas. It's too dangerous."

"How would she know that? She isn't even real."

"Mom, please listen. This is what she said." Holly continued to explain in detail what Felicity reported.

"I see. You really believe this, honey?"

"Yes, Mom, I do. Everything she has told us so far has come true. Please believe me. I don't want anything to happen to you or Dad."

"Okay, honey. Nothing is going to happen to us. Now let's talk about more pleasant things. We have twelve more days before we have to leave. Let's spend them doing some fun things. I don't want to think about this warning again. It is all part of your dream and not real."

Holly shook her head as tears began to bead. "Mom, please don't dismiss this. It's a matter of life or death."

"Honey, please don't get upset. I'll discuss this with your father. Now let's walk a little longer then go back home. How would you like to go to a movie? You pick one and we can go with Abby and Aunt Jane. Okay?"

Holly wiped her eyes with the back of her hand and nodded, "Okay."

She felt happy that her mother wanted to go, but at the same time unsettled over not being able to convince her mother of the dire warning. Holly would have to talk to Abby and see what their next move would be. Maybe she had better luck with Aunt Jane.

When they arrived back at the house, Abby and Jane were in the den with their heads together in deep conversation.

They looked up when they saw Holly and Shirley come into the room. Abby noticed that neither Holly nor her mother looked happy. Evidently the discussion didn't go well.

Shirley announced, "We are going to take in a movie. Who wants to go with us?" She looked over the girls' heads to lock eyes with her sister.

"Sure, that's a great idea. Let's go see what's up, Shirley." Jane responded and ushered her sister out of the den to go look up the movies and ask her what that look was about.

Abby and Holly were relieved that they were alone to discuss what happened when they told their mothers about Felicity's warning.

"What did your mother say, Holly?"

"She didn't believe me. She thought it was only a dream."

"Oh, I see."

"What did your mother say about it?"

"She is beginning to believe me about Felicity. She told me something that surprised me."

"What? What did she tell you?"

"Well, remember she came into our room the other day and was looking up at the ceiling. Evidently she saw Felicity or what she thought was a ghost."

"Really? Oh boy, Felicity is now appearing to your mother. Will she appear to my mother to convince her too? That might be the only way that she will believe me."

"Maybe it's time that we meet face to face with Felicity to discuss what we can do to convince my mother of the danger."

"How do we get her to come to us?
Are you up for a little nap, Holly?"

CHAPTER SEVEN

A Ghostly Visit

Abby and Holly told their mothers that they needed to go upstairs for a little while and freshen up before going to the movies.

"Sure honey. Go ahead. We'll let you know what's up and what time we'll be going. It will be your choice." Jane went back to looking at her phone for the times of the movies.

"What's going on with the girls, Jane?"

"What do you mean? Oh, the ghost visits you're talking about?"

"Yes, Holly told me about the warning that this so-called ghost, Felicity, told her about Jay and me."

"What do you think about this? Am I hurting my daughter by going away again? Is she making this up just to keep us from leaving?"

"That's a tough question or I should say questions, Shirl. It's not for me to tell you not to go. You need to make up your own mind about that. I know what I would do if I were in your position."

"Yeah, I know what you would do too. First of all, you wouldn't have gone at all. But it's not just Holly I have to think about. It's also Jay. This is his life's work. I need to think of him too. Holly is fine with you for another six months. After that time I will convince Jay that we need to stay here."

"Shirley, you need to think of your daughter now. She has been upset. You haven't seen her and how she reacts when you leave. You can't do that to her again." Jane couldn't help being angry with her sister.

"I agree with you, Sis. But I don't know how to tell Jay that I don't want to go back with him. He will think that I don't want to support him anymore."

"Listen, you are two grownups. You can discuss this and come to a consensus. Let him go back alone to finish up his duties. You need to stay here with your daughter."

"Does that mean you don't believe what Holly said about the ghost's warning about the danger of going back?"

"Well, I am beginning to believe this ghost business. I…never mind. You need to discuss this with Jay. I will support you in whatever you decide to do." Jane whispered under her breath, *I hope you decide to stay.*

"What did you say, Jane?"

"Oh nothing, Shirl. It's all good. Talk to Jay. Let's make a list of the movies and times and tell the girls. It would do us good to get out – girls' day out."

"Okay. Let me go freshen up. Be ready in a sec."

Jane watched her sister go upstairs to her room. She followed behind but went into the girls' room to share the movies and times.

"Hey girls, what are you in the mood for? Comedy, adventure, suspense?"

Jane stopped in her tracks as she looked above the girls' bed.

The girls were laying down taking a nap. Hovering over them was a phantom. The phantom turned to focus on her when she heard Jane's voice.

Jane backed away but stopped when the ghost spoke to her.

Please don't leave.

There is something you need to know.

You must convince your sister not to go.

Danger is close by.

They must not fly.

Jane spoke up, her shaky voice displaying her shock.

"I don't know what to say to her. How do you know this? Are you real or am I imagining this?"

I am a specter, a ghost or phantom, whatever you want to call me.

I know things that you cannot possibly know.

I have connections from the other side.

Believe me when I say, they must not GO!

Jane felt cold all over, goosebumps forming on her arms. She still couldn't move.

"I…I will do my best to convince her. Please don't harm us."

I will never harm anyone.

I must go now.

Heed my warning, Jane.

Jane rushed over to the bed and woke the girls. She explained what she saw and heard.

"Oh, my God, Mom. Felicity appeared to you. I can't believe it. She is serious about this. Now do you believe us?"

Jane stood transfixed and shaky as she responded, "Yes...I must tell Shirley. She can't leave."

"Let's go tell Mom now, Aunt Jane."

The three moved together up one more flight to Shirley's and Jay's room. They knocked but no one answered. They tiptoed in and stood unable to move as they observed Felicity speaking to Shirley as she slept.

Felicity looked at them and smiled as only a ghost can smile. It's more of a feeling that she smiled. She had a face in a white wispy circle with holes where her eyes and mouth would be and flowing white hair. Felicity floated away up to the ceiling and disappeared from sight.

Jane shook Shirley awake and waited for her to say something.

"What, what happened? I laid down for just a minute then I saw a…I saw something. Was it a ghost? Was it Felicity? She came to me in a dream. Is this what you saw, Holly? She told me about the warning. Is this real? I don't know what to think? How could this happen?"

Holly sat on the bed next to her mother and hugged her tight. "Yes, Mom, she's real, as real as a ghost can be. She knew you didn't believe me. You have to believe me and her now."

"Yes, honey. I believe something happened and maybe this is a warning that I must heed. I will tell your father that we are not going. We'll work it out with Miracles Across Borders. They will accept our decision because of my health as the reason."

"Oh Mom, thank you so much! Thank you! I love you!" Holly hugged and cried with her mother as

Jane hugged Abby and joined in with their own tears.

Later that night Shirley relayed what she had heard in her dream and what Holly had told her. Jay sat there stumped as to what to say in response. He was concerned that both his daughter and his wife were going crazy.

He knew he couldn't get out of the contract with Miracles Across Borders but understood about his wife's health keeping her from going.

"Okay, honey. I believe you. Everything is going to be all right. Your health is more important. I agree, you should not be going. We can get a doctor's note. Why don't you rest now? I don't want you to get over-exerted and stressed by all this."

He tucked his wife into bed and went to take a shower. He did his best thinking in the shower.

Half an hour later he had a plan. He made up his mind then and there that he would go back and fulfill his duties and leave his wife behind. He didn't plan on telling anyone until it was time for him to leave. It was better that way. He had a job to do and never left a job unfinished.

In time they would understand. He only hoped they would forgive him.

CHAPTER EIGHT

Popcorn and Movies

The next morning everyone was in better spirits. The girls never made it to the movies because of the phantoms visit the previous day. They all decided to go that afternoon and see the latest adventure movie, have plenty of popcorn, candy and whatever else they could eat. They even decided to make a complete day of it and go out to dinner later that evening.

It was a celebration of sorts for all. Jane was thrilled that her sister would be staying home for good. Holly was ecstatic that she would have her mother around daily. Abby was happy for her cousin that she would now smile more, be relaxed and no longer feel nervous. Bob was relieved that he didn't have to hear from his wife any more about how Shirley was neglecting her daughter.

Jay was the only one that was quiet and introspective. No one noticed this because of their own exuberant feelings.

Everyone enjoyed the movie, ate plenty of popcorn, soda or water and red licorice sticks. On the way home, they were too full or they would have stopped for ice cream to keep the celebration going.

Abby suggested, "Why don't we get an ice cream after dinner tonight. We can stop by Mini's Ice Cream Stand near your favorite restaurant, Mom and Dad."

"We'll see how hungry you are after a big meal. You probably won't want anything else."

"Well, okay. You never know though, I have a good appetite. There's always room for ice cream," Abby chuckled.

Holly bumped shoulders with her cousin and joined in laughing over her sense of humor. Abby was known to be able to eat tons of ice cream and not gain an ounce.

Holly looked at her mother and father sitting across from her and Abby in Uncle Bob's SUV. Uncle Bob's job as a manager of a home improvement store enabled him to have this special updated van and use it for personal use too. The seats could be turned to face each other or face forward.

Holly's parents were both serious and quiet. In fact, they hadn't said anything all the way home from the movies. Something was not right here. Holly tried to open a dialogue with them.

"What did you think of the movie, Mom and Dad?"

"It was good," her mother responded.

"Yeah, good movie," her dad remarked.

Abby broke in to relieve the tension, "Let's ride our bikes when we get back. Maybe we can go to the park and hang out there on the swings. What do you say, Holly? It's still early enough before we go out for dinner."

"Huh, maybe." Holly barely listened for she was looking at her parents who were unusually solemn.

Jane could feel the tension from her front row seat. She added, "I could go for a cup of coffee. Anybody interested?"

Bob answered, "Count me in, honey. I need to wash all the popcorn and candy away. We will have to wait a while before we go out to dinner. I'm still stuffed."

"I agree, Bob. It's early though. You girls can go for a short bike ride and then head back here by 5:30. I will call for a reservation for 7:00. That should give us enough time to change and get ready to go. Does everyone want to go to Angelo's?"

Abby jumped in, "Yes! I love their pasta and meatballs and eggplant parmigiana. It's almost as good as yours, Mom."

"Ha-ha, thanks, honey."

"Is this okay with you, Sis and Jay?"

An interminable time passed before Shirley answered, "Sure that sounds fine, Jane."

"Is everything okay back there? Do you feel too tired to go, Shirl? If you do, I can cook something and we can go out another night."

"No, I'm feeling well. Don't worry about me. Let's make it tonight. Right, Jay?"

"Huh, oh, right. Tonight's good."

Holly sighed when her parents were not responding in a normal way. She would have to talk to her mother after they got home. She was hiding something and her parents' sullen attitude didn't indicate a positive thing.

***

Holly followed her mother into the house and tapped her on the arm before she could escape up to her room. "Hey Mom, can we talk?"

"Sure honey. Are you okay?"

"That's what I wanted to ask you and Dad. You both were awfully quiet on the way home. Is anything wrong?"

"No, honey. Everything is fine. In fact, I am a little tired but feeling much better today."

"Well, I'm relieved to hear that, Mom. What about Dad. Is he feeling okay? His expression was one of something heavy on his mind. Is he getting second thoughts about not going back with the Miracles Across Borders?"

"He hasn't talked about it since we made the decision not to go back. Maybe he's just disappointed about not being able to complete his commitment. Don't worry, honey. He'll get used to the idea. He may even like being here so we can go looking for a house of our own."

"But Mom, I thought we were going to live here with Aunt Jane and Uncle Bob and Abby."

"Well, Holly we can't impose on them forever. We need to have our own space. We'll stay here temporarily until we find a place. Now, I need to go lay down for a little while before we go out for dinner."

Holly hung her head and walked away to tell Abby what her mother said.

Abby met Holly halfway to the garage door to get their bikes. She took one look at Holly's face and knew something had upset her. She could see tears threatening to fall.

"What's wrong, Holly? Is your mom okay?"

"Yeah, she's okay but she said we're going to be moving once we find our own house."

"What? Why does she want to do that? There's plenty of room here for the three of you!"

"I know, but she insists that we move. Maybe it was my Dad's idea. My mom loves to be with your mom. I guess Dad needs his own space. He's funny like that. He doesn't have any family and doesn't know how to socialize. He is too serious most of the time. I wish he knew how to have fun like your dad does."

"Maybe he's having second thoughts about quitting his job. He then has to find another job here. He's probably worried about affording everything and doesn't want to take advantage of our hospitality."

"Yeah, that's probably it. I hope he doesn't find a house too soon. I don't want to leave you, Abby!"

"Don't worry my mom will convince them to stay. Let's take a ride. It'll do you good to get some exercise. Now stop the tears. You know what I said about the cost of tissues." Abby urged as she jumped on her bike, opened the garage door and raced away.

"Hey, wait for me!" Holly yelled feeling better after talking to her best friend.

***

Dinner at Angelo's was delicious as always. Everyone was in good spirits and conversation was nil as they devoured plates of chicken and eggplant parmigiana, meatballs, spaghetti and antipasto.

Abby convinced everyone to stop by Mini's Ice Cream before heading home much to their chagrin and full stomachs.

Any worries were forgotten for now but would surface soon enough.

CHAPTER NINE

Twelve Days Later

"Honey, what's been bothering you?" Shirley looked at her husband's handsome face as he got dressed.

Jay yawned as he brushed his blonde hair into place. "What did you say, Shirl?"

"Well, you look worried about something. What's bothering you?"

"Umm, nothing's bothering me, honey. Are you feeling better?"

"Yes, I am, Jay. I'm feeling a lot better. I guess it was all the rest I've been getting over many days. Also, my sister won't let me do anything around here. I only clean our room and bathroom because I insisted on doing at least that much."

"Hmm, that's good."

Shirley touched Jay on the arm to stop him as he passed by her. She put her arms around his neck when he turned toward her and kissed him soundly.

"What was that for, Shirl?"

"I love you, Jay. Don't you like it?" she smiled as she gave him another hug.

"I love you too, honey. I'm fine. Don't worry about anything. I'm relieved that you are better and rested. I guess the whole idea of traveling and medically caring for the underprivileged was too much for you."

"Not really, Jay. It was my own neglect in forgetting to take my injections of insulin. Are you upset about not completing our agreement with Miracles Across Borders?"

"No, but let's not talk about this now. Okay? Jane and Bob are waiting for us at breakfast. We'll talk later."

"Okay, but we need to talk about it. You never told me what they said about us quitting the program."

Jay didn't answer and headed downstairs before Shirley asked him any more questions. He sighed as he sat down at the table to eat.

Jane and Bob looked up as Shirley and Jay said, "Good morning everyone."

"Hey good morning to you too. You are looking much better each day, Sis!"

"I'm feeling better too. Thanks, Jane. You've been making me lazy around here. I can start doing some housework and cooking to help you out."

"Well, I may let you do a little cooking now and then. I like your chili, pot roast, and spareribs."

"Oh you do? Well, let me make one of them tonight. I can go shopping if you let me use your car. It's a warm day perfect for some ribs on the grill."

Bob's ears perked up when he heard ribs. "Yeah, I am in for the ribs. I'll even cook them on the grill if you marinate them or whatever you do, Shirl."

Abby and Holly walked in on the conversation but heard ribs. "Ribs, yeah we want ribs, don't we, Holly?"

"Oh yeah! I love my Mom's ribs. Are you cooking, Mom?"

"Yes, I am. Okay, ribs it is. I'll make baked potatoes and tossed salad too."

"Sounds good to me," Jane said and added, "We can go shopping right after breakfast."

"Hey girls, eat up. Your bus is almost here. You only have another week of school left."

"I know, I can't believe it!" Abby bounced down on her chair and attacked her egg and cheese sandwich.

Holly licked the yolk that ran out of her sandwich onto her fingers. "This is delicious, Aunt Jane."

"Glad you like it, Holly."

"Do you have much to do this week in school, Holly?" her mother inquired.

"Not really, Mom. We're doing cleaning in the classrooms and clearing out our lockers. We may watch a movie too."

"That's good. We'll have a fun summer together."

"I can't wait, Mom." Holly gulped down the rest of her sandwich when Abby poked her to get a move on. The bus would be coming soon.

The girls cleaned up their area on the table and themselves. After hugs and kisses around the girls ran out the door to meet the bus at the corner.

Bob excused himself and said his goodbyes as he headed to work with a heavy briefcase.

Shirley turned toward Jay who was sitting alone drinking a second cup of coffee, "You don't mind if I go shopping do you, Jay? What are you going to do today?"

Jay didn't answer but hung his head before answering, "I'm going back."

Shirley stopped clearing the table and nearly dropped her coffee cup when she heard Jay's response.

"What do you mean, you're going back?"

"Just that, Shirl. One of us has to fulfill this obligation to these people and to the group. I didn't tell them I wasn't going to return. I only told them that you couldn't come with me because of health reasons."

"But why, Jay? We agreed on this that you wouldn't be going without me. It's over for both of us." Shirley turned away from him as tears rimmed her eyes.

Jane quietly slipped out unannounced to give her sister and brother-in-law some much needed privacy.

"No Shirl, it isn't over for me, not yet. I will complete the six months remaining and then come back. You have to understand. I can't leave all those sick people in the lurch. I am a doctor first and foremost." Jay drained the rest of his coffee and left the room.

Following behind him, Shirley continued, "What about Holly and me? You are also a husband and father. Did you forget that?" Shirley was now crying so hard that she choked on her words and couldn't finish.

Jay stopped at the foot of the stairs. "No I didn't forget about you or Holly. I am doing this for both of you. What would you think of me if I didn't complete my obligations?" He continued up the stairs.

"Jay, don't leave. We need to discuss this more. You can't go back." Shirley's shoulders were shaking and she covered her face in her hands and went back and sat down at the table.

Jane rushed over to her and hugged her from behind. "It's okay, Shirl. He'll come to his senses. Don't worry. He won't leave you. Jay's a good man. It must be tough for him not to complete this tour."

"I know, Jane. But he can't go. He has to stay with us. What am I going to do without him?"

"You are going to stay here with us. You will always have a home here whether Jay stays or goes. Your place is here."

Shirley continued to cry as Jane handed her tissue after tissue to stop the flow of her tears.

"Now go upstairs and talk to him some more. I'll clean up. When you're ready, come down and we'll go shopping. Okay?"

"Okay. Thanks, Sis. You're the best. I wouldn't know what to do without you."

"That's what sisters are for, remember we are almost twins and always good friends."

Shirley smiled remembering they always said that when they were young.

Jane puttered around the kitchen and then started the laundry. When after an hour had passed and Shirley had not come back, Jane walked up to her room and knocked on the door.

She could hear sniffling and opening and shutting of drawers. The door opened to her sister's blotchy face and runny nose.

"I'm sorry, Shirley, but I was getting worried. Is everything all right?"

"No, Jay is packing and leaving tonight. I can't convince him to stay. He's made up his mind."

"Oh, Shirley, I'm sorry. What can I do to help? Do you want me to talk to him?"

"No, he won't listen to anyone. He's too stubborn and won't change his mind. He said he'll talk to Holly when she comes home and leave right after dinner. He has a flight at 8:30 pm."

"Okay, I'll have dinner ready at 5:30. It only takes thirty minutes to get to the airport from here."

"I'll prepare dinner, Jane. Did you forget already? I'm ready to go shopping now. Let me wash my face and put on some makeup to cover my blotches."

"Sure, I'll be downstairs whenever you're ready."

Shirley looked back at Jay as she opened the door of their room. I'll see you later, Jay."

"Okay, Shirl. Please try to understand."

Shirley shook her head and left before her tears started flowing again.

CHAPTER TEN

An Unhappy Announcement

The girls were clearing out the last vestiges of junk in their lockers when the bell sounded ending the school day.

"Wow, how come the last week of school each day flies by? All year long each day drags," Holly sighed.

"Got me, Cuz. I like these days. We get to have fun watching movies and not so much cleaning out our desks and lockers. Ugh!" Abby scrunched up her face.

"Yeah. We can even talk all day long. The teacher is too preoccupied cleaning out her desk and covering her shelves with paper to pay attention to us." Holly grabbed the last of her stuff from her locker and shoved it into her backpack.

The girls headed to the bus and lined up behind several other students. Their conversation continued all the way home.

"What are we going to do for the rest of the week? We've already cleaned out our desks and lockers."

"We can help the teacher cover her shelves with paper," Abby giggled.

"Huh, oh right! Like you want to do that."

"Don't you, Holly? I know how you need to keep busy."

"No, I don't think so, Abby. I'll find something to do. We can bring in a book to read. I've got a couple I wanted to read for the summer but I can get a head start. Or even better I can begin my own story."

"Ok, that sounds good, but I'm bringing in my drawing pad to create some new clothes. I can make something for both of us."

"Hmm, that would be great, Abby. What are you going to draw for me? How about a pair of shorts and top?"

"Oh, that would be too plain. I'll come up with something special that no one else has. We may start a trend."

"Wow, do you think so? That would be so cool."

At their stop the girls rushed down the stairs and walked quickly back to Abby's house. Outside in the driveway were their mothers who were busy removing groceries from the trunk of the car.

"Hey Mom. Do you need help?" Abby slipped on her backpack to free her hands and grabbed a couple of bags. Holly followed behind her and took two more.

"Thanks, girls. We did buy a little more than I expected. That's what happens when we go together, huh, Shirl?"

"I guess so, Jane." Shirley rushed into the house with the last two bags and dropped them onto the counter then quickly headed upstairs before Holly noticed her still blotchy face.

"Where are you going, Mom?"

"I'll be right back, Holly. I need to talk to your father for a minute."

Abby exchanged looks with her mother as Holly followed her mother upstairs.

"What's wrong, Mom? I saw Aunt Shirley's red nose and blotchy cheeks. She's been crying."

"You better stop your cousin from going to her parents' room, Abby."

"Why, Mom? Please tell me."

"No, Holly needs to hear it from her parents. Now, go stop her. You'll learn what's going on soon enough."

"Okay. I'll be right back." Abby ran up the stairs and caught Holly before she knocked on her parents' door.

"Hey where are you going in such a hurry? Is there a fire or something?"

"No, don't bother your parents. Come downstairs and help me put away the groceries. That's my mom's order."

"I will in a minute after I see my parents. Something is wrong. My mother raced away and didn't even look at me."

"I noticed that too, Holly. But let them come down and talk to you."

"Talk to me, about what?" Holly's face blanched.

"I don't know. My mother wouldn't tell me. There's something wrong though. I can feel it too, Holly."

"Oh God, maybe my mom is sick again," Holly reached forward and knocked on the door.

Shirley opened the door a crack and peeked out. "Holly, what's wrong, honey?"

Holly's eyes filled and she hugged her mother as soon as she opened the door wider.

"Why are you crying, Holly? Did Aunt Jane tell you?"

"No, she didn't tell me anything. I know something is wrong. You never looked at me when I came home, and ran away to your room. Why, Mom?"

"Come in and sit down, Holly. Your dad and I have something to tell you."

Jay stepped away from his suitcase and sat next to Holly on the queen-sized bed.

Holly could see the bed was covered with clothes and a half-filled suitcase.

"Where are you going, Dad?"

Jay cleared his throat and got right into the subject, "Listen, Holly. I need to go back to finish up my term with Miracles Across Borders."

"What? Why, Dad? Is Mom going with you?"

"No, Mom is not going. But I need to finish up my obligation."

Shirley came and put her arms around her daughter as she openly cried.

"I don't understand, Dad. I thought you were both staying home now. You don't need to go, do you?"

"Yes, Holly, I do. This is a written obligation that I must complete. Your mother is excused because of health reasons. I don't have that excuse. They expect me to go back. It'll be only for six months then I'll be back for good."

Holly sniffled, wiped her tears and blew her nose before responding, "I can see how you need to do this, Dad. But what about us? We'll be without you for six months. Also, what about the warning?"

"Yes, but you have each other, and your aunt and uncle will let you stay here until I get back. Stop about that ghost nonsense. When I return we will find our own place. Okay?"

"But Dad, I don't want to leave here even after you return. Aunt Jane said she will fix up this floor for us. We will have our own apartment. I'm happy staying with Abby," Holly took a deep breath and continued, "and the warning isn't nonsense!"

"Holly, I'm not going to say it again. No more about this ghost nonsense, please. Staying here is temporary. We need to have our own space."

Holly continued to weep and got up from the bed and hugged her mother as they both cried.

Abby stayed outside the room but could hear everything being said. She went back downstairs to report to her mother.

"I heard Uncle Jay say he's going back. That's why Aunt Shirley was so upset. Also, Uncle Jay doesn't believe us about Felicity and her warning. He told Holly not to talk about the ghost nonsense anymore."

"Yes, honey. We're all upset over this. As for the ghost, it is hard even for me to believe after hearing and seeing her."

"But Uncle Jay said he's going to look for a home for them when he returns. He can't take Holly away. We've become like sisters. I can't lose her."

"I know, Abby. Now help me put away the rest of the groceries before they spoil. We won't worry about this now. It won't happen for another six months. He may change his mind by then."

"Will you fix up the third floor for them in the meantime?"

"Yes we plan to do just that so my sister and niece can have a place of their own."

"Okay. That makes me feel better."

But Abby sighed heavily and knew that things were going to change when Uncle Jay returned. She only hoped that Felicity was wrong about the dangers ahead.

CHAPTER ELEVEN

Last Day of School

Now that school was finishing today Holly tried to accept that her father would not be coming back for six months. She and her mother were going to keep busy taking walks, shopping, going to the movies and spending days together talking.

Jane and Bob were busy fixing up the third floor to include a kitchen and living room. There were four bedrooms and three bathrooms there. One bedroom was already refurbished for Jay and Shirley and another one would be for Holly. The other two larger bedrooms were being used to accommodate the kitchen and living rooms. One of the three bathrooms was being used to include a laundry room. Everything was planned out with Bob doing as much work as he could on the project. He had a plumber and an electrician to do the parts he wasn't able to do.

***

The girls finished up school with little fanfare and headed home on the bus.

They made plans to spend time with other friends and spoke to Davey and Derek Donato, the twin detectives, about going to the movies some time.

"See you later, girls. We'll call you about the times of the movies. You can let us know what you prefer to see. Okay?" Davey queried as he got to his stop.

"Sure, sounds good, Davey," Abby countered.

Derek added, "Yeah, see you later girls. I think there's some blockbuster movies coming this summer. I'll see whatever you chose. Okay?" He smiled at Holly and hopped off the bus.

Holly blushed and waved at Derek as Abby did the same to Davey.

The girls both sighed and smiled at each other as they got off at their stop and skipped lightheartedly on their way home.

Hammering and sawing could be heard as they got closer to home. A large pod to hold the old furniture from the rooms being worked on was outside the house along with a long and deep bin to collect the trash.

The girls were excited to see what had been done to the apartment. They came through the hall and yelled out, "Hi, we're home!"

"Hey there. How was the last day of school?" Jane wiped her hands on her

apron as she came out to greet the
girls.

"Great, it's over, Mom! What else
can I say?"

"Yeah, it's finally over! Phew! Now
the fun begins!" Holly did a happy
dance.

Shirley smiled wide and opened her
arms to her daughter to envelop her in
a huge hug.

"It's good to have you both home.
We were outside sitting on the patio
having an iced tea. Do you girls want
one? I'll get some snacks too."

"Yeah, sure. We want to get some
shorts and tees on first. We'll be right
back."

"Stay out of your father's way on the third floor. He's knee deep in sawdust and cobwebs."

"Ugh, sure thing, Mom!" Abby made faces at Holly.

"I hate spiders, Abby. Let's not go upstairs right now. We can check it out later after it's cleaned."

"Yeah, I agree. Race you to our room."

The cousins giggled and pushed each other and bumped their way to their room.

Outside on the colored stone patio, which had been redone by Bob when they first came to the house, was a lovely comfy set of outdoor furniture, a couch, four chairs and a small round coffee table. The couch and chairs had cushions that were soft and brightly colored. There was a long rectangular table with eight chairs around and each had a puffy cushion that matched the ones on the couch and lawn chairs.

There was a six-foot stockade fence encircling the expansive yard and a small pond nearby with a waterfall that gurgled making for a relaxing time as they listened to it.

Jane and Bob had done most of the work themselves with a little help from a stone mason for the pond and the area with the grill and stone wall that lined the back of the patio to separate it from the sitting area.

It had become their little oasis away from stress and daily problems.

Jane glanced over at her sister who had her eyes closed as she sipped the iced tea. She could hear a sigh escape Shirley's lips every so often which made her smile.

The girls came back and sat down on the last two lawn chairs with glasses of iced tea in their hands.

"Ah, this is the life, huh Mom?" Abby sighed as she stretched out her slim frame.

"Yes, it is, honey. The yard looks good, doesn't it, Abby?"

"It looks great, Mom. I did a perfect job of weeding last week."

"Wait a minute, I helped too," Holly chirped in with a chuckle.

"Oops, sorry, Cuz! I forgot." Abby giggled as she smirked at Holly.

"Yes, I agree. You both did a commendable job," Shirley added with a satisfied grin of her own.

"Oh you girls, always joking. But I have to admit you are good workers. Speaking of that, now that you are all done with school you can take on some chores."

A few moans and groans were heard but quickly stifled as Jane met the girls' eyes.

"Only kidding, Mom. Sure, what do you need?"

"Ah, that's better. I will leave a list on the fridge for you both to tackle beginning tomorrow. Okay?"

Holly spoke up, "Anything you need we can handle, Aunt Jane. I'm happy to be here and now that you're fixing upstairs for us I can't thank you enough."

"It's my pleasure, Holly dear. Anything for you and your mom to keep you here."

Shirley opened her eyes and sat up. "Oh Jane, I don't want you to get your hopes up too much. You know Jay. He may want to move once he gets back."

"Now, let's not think about this okay? Once he sees the finished apartment he will not want to leave. It'll be beautiful and the rent cheap."

Shirley laughed at that last statement and relaxed once again and lay back on the chaise.

"Do you girls want to go shopping tomorrow after you finish your chores?" Jane interrupted their thoughts.

"Huh? Shopping? Sure, Mom. I always love shopping. What are we shopping for?"

Jane and Shirley both smiled and nodded to each other. "We are going to choose some furniture for the third floor, a living room set, kitchen appliances, and a bed for your new room."

"My new room? I thought I was going to stay with Abby in her room."

"Well, we are fixing up the second bedroom on the third floor for you. You can pick out all your own stuff."

"Oh, well, maybe," Holly's eyes got big at the thought of new stuff for her own bedroom.

Abby hung her head and didn't say a word.

When Holly saw Abby's dejected expression she said, "Oh never mind. I like being in Abby's room."

Abby lifted her face and smiled at Holly but added, "Wait a minute, Holly. We could take turns staying with each other in our rooms. It would be fun like a sleepover. I'll help you pick out some cool things too!"

"Okay, that sounds great, Abby! I'll share my stuff with you too."

"Oh perfect! That's sounds good to me." The girls giggled as they conspired what to buy to furnish this new bedroom that they would use together.

"I'm starving, Mom. What do we have for snacks?"

Jane brought the tray of goodies closer so they could sample them as she and Shirley sighed in relief.

***

Shirley didn't want to leave this beautiful house any more than her daughter did. She knew she would have to convince her husband of that one day when he returned. She was beginning to like this arrangement and being with her sister every day. Also, she could see how happy Holly was to be with her cousin.

Shirley knew that she would have to go looking for a job soon to help out around the house with expenses. She planned on paying rent no matter what her sister said. But for now she wanted to enjoy being jobless and spending time with Holly as much as she could to make up for the lost time.

CHAPTER TWELVE

sweep patio
vacuum rugs
wash dishes
set table
do laundry

Chores Time

The girls were up early and ready to take on the chores that Jane had assigned them. They sat at breakfast and discussed what they would do after the chores were done.

"Holly, what if we take a long bike ride to the lake. We can wear our swimsuits under our shorts and tees and pack towels and a lunch. I'm sure there's something we can scrounge up in the fridge."

"Okay, that sounds great but we need to check with our mothers first. They may not want us to venture that far on our bikes."

"All right, wait a minute. I'll take care of that," Abby stopped in mid-stream and called out to her mother, "Hey Mom, can Holly and I go to the lake on our bikes today?"

"That's a long way, honey. We could all go together in the car. I'll even pack a nice lunch for us and then we can picnic there and get ice cream on the way home from Mini's."

Holly smiled now realizing that this was Abby's plan all along. They would ride there in the car and even get ice cream too. Not a bad plan at all, she giggled thinking about it.

"What's so funny, Holly?" Shirley studied her daughter's animated face.

"Oh nothing. I'm just excited about us all going to the lake. It'll be fun. We haven't gone there with you, Mom. You'll love it."

"I'm sure I will. But you do remember I was a kid once and did go to lakes back then."

"Yeah, but not to Meadow Lake, Mom. It has a platform to swim to with a ladder to climb up and then jump off or take the slide down. It's so cool!"

"Oh, I see. That does sound pretty cool," Shirley chuckled at her daughter's exuberance.

"But before we can go, you girls have to complete all your chores," Jane added with a smile.

"Of course, Mom. We will." Abby nodded at Holly who jumped up after finishing her breakfast to clear the table and wash the dishes which was one of her chores."

Abby headed to the laundry room to put in a load of laundry before going to clean the half bath down the hall.

Since there were so many bathrooms, seven in all, four of which were in working order, in this house the girls took turns cleaning them along with their mothers. The girls were expected to clean their own bathroom and bedroom year round though.

After each chore was completed the girls would go back to the list on the refrigerator to check them off.

"Almost there, Abby. I have two more chores to do. How about you?"

"I've got two more too. I need to sweep the patio and vacuum the den and living rooms."

"That's not too bad. I have to vacuum the second floor rooms and wash the bathroom floors up there. My mom said not to worry about the third floor. It's in a mess right now. Your dad is cleaning up and then stopping for a break. He's been working all morning and worked late into the night last night."

"He really wants to get this done. He can only do it after work each day. We should sneak up after he's done cleaning and take a peek."

"Yeah, we haven't seen it since he started. Mom talked us out of going up yesterday because of the spiders and cobwebs."

"Let's do it. Hurry and finish up your work then we can go up there."

After the last chore was completed the girls tiptoed up to the third floor and opened the door to the hall. It was eerily quiet.

The electrician had been there the day before to install lights in the halls and in the rooms making it easier to see their way down the long corridor.

"Wow, this is really something. I can't believe this house. It's almost as if it is growing each time I look at it. Our room is bigger too. Didn't you notice that, Abby?"

"Now that you say that, I agree. I did notice it was roomier. We have more space to put our stuff. But how could that be? Houses can't grow, can they?"

"Hmm, good question. Look at this, Abby! It's our kitchen with cabinets and everything. Wow, this living room is large enough to have a pool table and some pinball machines and stuff like Davey and Derek have in their basement."

"Yeah, it is huge. You can have a big screen TV and two couches, two chairs, a coffee table and still have room. Wow, so cool!"

"Your dad has done a beautiful job clearing out all the clutter that was here by the looks of what's in the trash bins outside."

"Yes, he has. He's handy and can do anything. I'm lucky to have such a special dad," Abby sighed with a smile.

"I agree, Abby. You are lucky. My dad doesn't do all this stuff. He can't injure his hands. He's a doctor and needs to keep his hands in good shape. That's what he tells me each time I ask him to build a bookcase for all my books."

"No problem, my dad will build us one for each of our rooms," Abby mused thinking that soon they would have two bedrooms to share.

"That's right, we will have two bedrooms to store all our stuff. How cool is that, Abby?"

"Too cool to imagine, Holly!"

"What was that? Did you hear that? It sounds like it's coming from the other room outside my parent's room."

"Let's go see. It's a bathroom and laundry area, Holly. Maybe the sink is dripping or something."

"I don't know. I thought it sounded like a voice. I heard a voice, Abby."

"Hmm, I didn't hear anything. Maybe it's Felicity. She's probably checking out the new place too."

Abby walked into the room and called out, "Felicity, is that you? It's Abby and Holly. Where are you?"

A willowy mist appeared in the corner of the room above the sink as the girls came closer to get a better look.

"Felicity, is that you?" Holly inquired.

CHAPTER THIRTEEN

A Ghostly Conversation

Holly stopped in her tracks and grabbed Abby's hand. "That isn't Felicity. Who is it?"

"I...I don't know, Holly. Who are you? What do you want? Why are you here?"

"Try asking it one question at a time, Abby. It's not going to answer all of them at once. Let me try."

"Who are you?"

I'm a friend of Felicity. She invited me to come over to live on this floor.

"What's your name?" Abby asked.

Minerva.

"How old are you, Minerva, or should I ask, how old were you when you passed?" Holly enquired.

I was fifteen when I died. I got sick with TB.

"Oh, I'm so sorry about that. It's nice to meet you Minerva," Abby responded in a sad voice.

Nice to meet you both too. Can I ask you a question?

"Of course you can. What is it?" Holly reacted.

Can I stay here now that this is all changed?

Abby and Holly exchanged worried glances before answering.

"I don't know. Maybe you can stay in the rooms behind the walls. Holly and her family will be staying here. Her parents wouldn't understand seeing you and may be frightened."

Oh, I see. I know people are afraid of me. I had to leave the last house because the people chased me away with a priest and a paranormal investigator. It wasn't fun being there with them.

Abby whispered into Holly's ear. "Why can't she stay here with you and your family? She will have to stay away when your parents are here and then hide in the walls most of the time. She can come out only when you call her."

"Yes, I think that would work. Let's ask her."

"Minerva, we've decided that you can stay here and be our ghost friend like Felicity. But you must promise never to appear when Holly's parents are around. You can live inside the walls where there is plenty of space and travel from my room to Holly's here. You can visit with your friend,

Felicity, easier that way, okay?"
Abby waited for Minerva to respond.

Okay, I guess. But all you have to do is whisper my name and I will hear you and come. This will be fun having more friends. Felicity told me all about you and said you are fun. I never had any friends when I was alive. Thank you for being my friends.

"We're happy to have you as our friend too, Minerva," Holly nodded to Abby and smiled.

"Can you tell us a little about you when you were alive, Minerva?" Abby enquired.

Oh, yes, I'm sorry. I should introduce myself better. I lived in that house, from which I was driven out, nearly

100 years ago on the other side of town. It's a large old house but not as large as this one. My grandmother lived with my mother, brother, sister and me. When my grandmother died my mother inherited the house but got sick with tuberculosis a few years later. Soon after I succumbed too. Before my mother died she left me and my siblings in the care of my aunt who lived in a neighboring town. She came to live in the house and tried to help me get better while caring for my brother and sister. But it was not to be and here I am.

"Oh, my, I'm so sorry to hear, Minerva," Abby sighed sadly.

"But now you have a new family, Abby and me," Holly smiled to ease the sadness from Minerva.

Yes, I am happy to have two new sisters as friends. Thank you. Maybe one day I will pass over and see my mother, brother, sister and relatives.

"Maybe one day you will. You just have to be ready to do that, Minerva. We'll tell you some time about the other ghosts we had in the house before," Abby added.

Okay, but I'm not ready to leave you girls yet. We just met and became friends. Besides, Felicity and I are best friends.

"That's right. Felicity, I'm sure, would really miss you, Minerva," Holly whispered.

Yes, I would miss her too!

Holly changed the subject and asked, "How do you like my new apartment, Minerva? Did my uncle frighten you with all the noise he has been making?"

It did surprise me at first but I have been watching him from up above on the ceiling. He didn't see me. He works hard.

"Yes, my father does, and he's a nice man too. I don't think he would kick you out of our house."

That's good to know. Thank you. How come you weren't frightened of me?

"We were frightened when we first saw Felicity. After all it was our first time seeing a ghost," Holly chuckled.

"Yes, Minerva, we were really frightened half to death. We didn't know that there would be ghosts in this house even when others told us so," Abby's face took on a grimace then turned into a smile after thinking about that time.

I'm sure Felicity didn't mean to frighten you. She is a kind person or I should say ghost. Bells were heard tinkling around Minerva.

Abby and Holly exchanged shocked expressions when they heard the sound and asked, "What was that, Minerva?"

Oh, that was my laugh. I don't have a real laugh anymore. But I can bring on bells to make it sound like I am laughing. Did they startle you?

"Yeah a little. We didn't expect that. How do you make bells ring?" Holly asked clearly intrigued.

Well, it's kind of a trick that I learned since I've been a ghost. I have connections to the other side and can request things from others.

Abby's eyes opened wider. "Really? What other things can you request, Minerva?"

Oh, I... a banging sound could be from heard behind them causing Minerva to stop talking and disappear.

"Hey girls, what are you doing up here? Be careful where you walk. I've got a lot more cleaning to do. How do you like it, Holly?"

"Oh, hi Dad. We didn't know you were still here. It looks great, huh Holly?"

Holly was looking around for the ghost. "Oh, yeah, Uncle Bob, it's fantastic! I love it! I can't wait for Mom and Dad to see this."

"Are you okay, Holly? You look pale like you've seen a ghost."

The girls' faces took on a serious expression then they roared with laughter and laughed until they cried. Bob stood there transfixed but didn't say anything but shake his head and walk away.

He could be heard mumbling to himself as he went downstairs.

"That was too funny, Abby. I can't believe your dad said that."

"I know. He doesn't even realize how true his words are. I couldn't help but laugh harder by the puzzled expression on his face. So funny, Holly!"

"Minerva, are you there?" Holly whispered.

Phew, that was a close call. I should have felt his presence but I was too busy chatting with my new friends, Minerva smiled as only a ghost can smile with a wispy streak.

"Can you tell us what you can request, Minerva? You didn't get a chance before," Abby inquired.

Well, I am connected to other spirits all over. There are many of us. But one particular one is the most powerful – that's Mianna. She controls most things for us. If we need something she can get it for us.

"Mianna? We know Mianna. She is our friends Davey's and Derek's Aunt Gigi's cat who lives inside her crystal ball." Abby couldn't keep still for she was jumping with excitement.

Holly clapped her hands in response. "Wow, that's incredible. You have connections with Mianna like Felicity does."

Abby gave Holly a hug and whispered in her ear, "Can you believe this? It gets better and better all the time. I love these ghosts."

Why do you do that? Whisper? I can still hear you when you do that, you know.

"You can? That's great, Minerva. We can whisper to you at night after we go to bed then our parents won't hear us talking to you."

"If you can hear us whisper, can you read our minds too?" Holly held her breath as she waited for a response from the ghost.

I can but only if you want me to. You can block me out of your mind just by saying, Block Minerva. Try it now.

Holly pursed her lips and said, "Block Minerva." as she thought up these words (blue, white and red).

Now unblock me and I will tell you what you are thinking. Go ahead, don't be afraid.

Abby watched in silence as Holly waited for Minerva to do her magic.

Blue, white and red

Holly gasped and grabbed Abby's hand in a squeeze. "I can't believe it. You can read minds. You're amazing, Minerva! Can Felicity do that too?"

I think all ghosts can do some things and not others. I'm not sure if Felicity can do that. But she can do other things that I can't do.

Abby couldn't contain her excitement once again and quickly asked, "What things can she do that you can't do?"

Oh, that is not for me to say. You should ask her about that some time. I need to go now, someone is coming.

Minerva, in a wispy puff of smoke, traveled up to the ceiling and then through the cracks in the wall to the secret passageways.

"Lovely, it's all so lovely, Bob. Thank you so much." Shirley's voice traveled from the other room.

The girls went back to the doorway of the laundry room and called out, "We're over here."

Shirley, Jane and Bob entered the laundry room where the girls had just spoken to Minerva.

"Isn't it wonderful, Mom?" Holly put her arms around her mother in a tight hug.

"Yes, honey, it's wonderful. I can't believe that your Uncle Bob did all this. I never looked outside of our bedroom. It was so dark and creepy. I was a little nervous coming up here every night. Who knows what's here."

Holly exchanged worried looks with Abby and covered up her surprise, "Do you believe in ghosts, Mom?"

Abby gasped, "Umm, Holly, there are no ghosts anymore. Remember they were exorcised by Davey and Derek."

"Oh yeah, that's right." Both girls looked at Bob who wore a puzzled expression as he puttered around the room looking at his handiwork for any mistakes.

Jane watched her daughter's face for some sign that she was hiding something. She and Shirley each already had a previous encounter with Felicity. They were now having serious doubts about those strange experiences.

"Why, Abby, did you see a ghost?"

"No Mom, we didn't. Why? What did Dad say to you?"

"Dad didn't say anything but I did hear him mumbling to himself as he came into the kitchen about girls being strange. What did he mean by that?"

"Oh, I don't know, Mom. Fathers can be odd at times," Abby giggled and punched Holly's arm and led her cousin out of the laundry room and back downstairs before her mother asked any more questions. She wanted to keep the new ghost a secret for now.

***

Later that afternoon the cousins and their mothers swam, picnicked and

enjoyed their day at Meadow Lake.
For now, the ghosts were forgotten.

CHAPTER FOURTEEN

Sharing Notes

"Holly, I can't believe all the spirits are connected to Mianna. Who would have thought that? Wow!"

"I know, it's amazing to think about. Each spirit has their own powers too. I want to ask Felicity what her special powers are but I think I already know."

"What? How would you know that, Holly?"

"Well, I remember she appeared with long hair and a face but Minerva only appears in a wisp of smoke or the shape of a face."

"Yes, that's right. I remember that too. But what else can she do?"

"We'll have to ask Felicity next time we see her, Abby."

The girls went downstairs to their shared room to see if they could conjure up Felicity.

"Felicity, are you there?" Abby whispered.

"Maybe she and Minerva are busy talking over things that we just discussed," Holly whispered back.

"Yeah, maybe." Abby turned suddenly and faced the secret door to the passageway in the wall.

"What's wrong, Abby? Did you see something?"

"No, but I thought I heard whispering from behind the door. Listen."

The girls put their ears on the door and waited.

"There, did you hear that, Holly?"

"Yes, I did hear something. It sounded like someone is whispering."

"Ha, it's Minerva talking to Felicity."

"How do you know, Abby?"

"Well, I just heard the bells tinkling –
her laugh."

"There it is again, Holly."

"Yes, yes, I did hear it that time. It
sounds like they are having a good
time."

"Let's whisper their names and see if
they can hear us."

Holly whispered as softly as she
could, "Minerva, Felicity, do you
hear me?"

Abby jumped in alarm away from the
door as two figures appeared – one a
willowy wisp of a cloud and the other
a ghost with white flowing hair and

facial features of a girl who was once pretty.

"Oh my. I didn't expect you to come so quickly," Abby's voice shook as she tried to stop shaking.

We're so sorry for frightening you like that, Abby. Are you all right?

"Oh, I'm fine now, Felicity. It's okay. I was startled, that's all." Abby smiled to put the ghosts at ease.

Holly giggled in relief after thinking over how Abby reacted to the ghosts' sudden appearance.

"What's so funny, Holly?"

"Oh nothing, Abby. I was remembering the expression on your startled face. It was funny."

"Well, you looked a little surprised yourself, Holly. In fact, your face is still a little pale."

Holly smirked and rubbed her cheeks to bring back the color. "Yeah, I guess I was a little shocked to see how fast Felicity and Minerva came when we whispered their names."

Yes, we did warn you that all you had to do was whisper our names and we would appear. A tinkling of bells was heard as Minerva drifted up to the ceiling to get comfortable.

Now Minerva, you better behave yourself. Remember you are a guest in Abby's house. She can send you away with just a word.

Oh, my, I do apologize, Abby and Holly. I really did not mean anything by that. Sorry I laughed. Please don't send me away, Felicity. I will be better.

"Oh, no, it's quite all right, Minerva. Please don't send her away, Felicity," Abby pleaded.

"Yes, she didn't do anything wrong. We were forewarned after all," Holly added.

Okay, this was just a warning to you, Minerva. You have been given another chance by Abby and Holly.

Oh, thank you so much, ladies. I am indebted to you. I wouldn't know where to go if I had to leave here. I

*am not welcome back at the other
house anymore.*

"But wait, you said I can send her
away. How can I do that, Felicity?"
Abby asked with a puzzled
expression.

*You have that power over us, Abby
and Holly. This is your house after
all. If you do not wish us to stay here
all you have to do is tell us to leave.*

Holly's face dropped in disbelief.
"Oh, we would never do that to either
of you."

Abby nodded in agreement and
stepped forward and asked, "Can I
give you a hug, Minerva? I think you
need one."

Minerva floated down from the ceiling and landed on Abby's arms. She encircled Abby's neck and gave her a squeeze."

"Oh, thank you, Minerva. I think I felt something touch me lightly." Abby responded and hugged the wisp back as much as she possibly could without pushing it away.

Thank you, Abby. I think I felt your hug too, a little. I sure do miss getting hugs when I was alive. I had a sister and brother who would hug me all the time. They were younger than I.

The girls heard a humming sound like a bee and hastily looked around to find it.

A familiar tinkling was once again heard as Minerva came close to the girls.

That was only me sighing. I requested a sound for my sighs too. I always loved bees and the sound they made, Minerva giggled.

"Okay, no problem, Minerva. We thought it was really a bee. I don't like to get stung. I swell up like crazy," Holly reported.

Oh Minerva, you are incorrigible, Felicity announced with her own sigh which sounded like a human sighing.

"Hey, Felicity, I actually heard you sigh. How come you have a real sigh?" Abby asked.

I wanted it to be like my own sigh when I was alive. It sounds pretty good, huh? Minerva laughed and a different sound was heard like a piano tune in high C.

"Wow, I love your laugh. It sounds like a piano in a high pitch," Holly proclaimed.

"There's so much we can learn from each other, Minerva and Felicity. I really enjoy talking with you both," Abby exclaimed with flushed cheeks.

The girls were so busy talking that they did not hear the footsteps coming into their room. They did notice that the ghosts disappeared through the cracks in the door panel as Jane and Shirley entered their daughters' room.

"Hey, where are you going?" Holly asked as she swiftly turned when she heard her mother's voice.

"We aren't going anywhere, honey. We came to see what you two were doing," Shirley answered unsure of what her daughter was up to.

"What's going on with you girls anyway?" Jane probed.

Abby countered, "Oh, nothing, Mom. We were just talking girl talk, that's all."

Holly looked up at the ceiling to check if the ghosts were observing them from above just before leaving their room. But they were not there.

Seeing Holly looking up, Jane and Shirley did the same and then looked at each other and shrugged.

The girls smiled prettily and headed out of the room and downstairs to get away before any more questions could be aimed at them.

With the girls out of earshot their mothers discussed their behavior. "What's with the girls, Shirl? Have you noticed that they are acting a little strange lately like they are hiding something from us?"

"Yes, I did notice that. But what are they hiding, Jane? Do you think it's about the twins, Davey and Derek?"

"Maybe, but I don't think so. Hmm. We'll have to keep a closer eye on them. Something is definitely up."

"Maybe it has something to do with the ghost, Felicity and her warning."

"Could be, Shirl, but I think it's something else. Well, we'll see."

CHAPER FIFTEEN

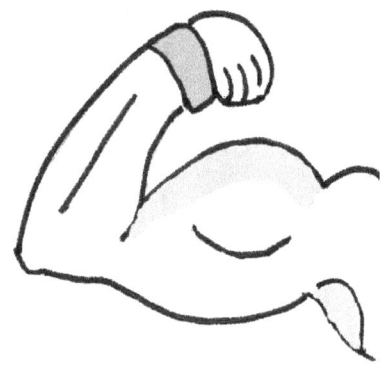

A Movie Date

Shirley and Jane were busy preparing dinner together when the phone rang. Being the closest to the wall phone Shirley picked it up.

"Hello."

"Umm, hi. Can I please speak to Abby?"

Shirley held the phone against her side and whispered to Jane about what the caller asked.

Jane relieved Shirley of the phone and asked, "Who is this?"

"Oh, hi Mrs. Rizzo? This is Davey Donato. I didn't recognize the other voice."

"Hi Davey. That's my sister, Holly's mother."

"Oh, I see. Can I speak to Abby please?"

"Of course, one moment while I call her."

"Abby, you have a phone call from Davey."

Holly jumped off the couch in the library and pulled Abby over to the phone extension on the table next to them.

"It's Davey, Abby. Hurry up and see what he wants."

"Hi Davey," Abby cleared her throat as she waited for him to say something.

"Hi Abby. Sorry to bother you. I hope you weren't busy."

"No, that's fine. Holly and I were just looking over some books in the library."

"Well, that's good. Umm, do you want to go to the movies tonight?"

"Really, a movie tonight? Wow, that would be awesome, Davey. Thank you!"

"Oh good, umm, there are two good movies up now – a super hero one and a mystery that also looks a little scary."

"I love super hero movies but if you want to see the scary mystery one I don't mind."

"No, the super hero one was my first choice too, but I wanted to give you first dibs, Abby."

"That's great, Davey. What time are you picking me up?"

"Well, the movie begins at 7:00 so I can pick you up...I mean my dad will pick you up, with me in the car of course, at about 6:15. That will give us some time to get our popcorn, drinks and snacks. Okay? But first Derek wants to talk to Holly," Davey chuckled at his own ineptitude.

Abby smiled excitedly and handed the phone to Holly after whispering, "Derek wants to talk to you!"

Holly's hands were shaking and she swallowed quickly before taking the phone and answering, "Hi Derek."

Davey was still on the line waiting for his brother. "Oh sorry, Holly. It's me Davey. Here's my brother."

"Hi Holly. Umm, do you want to go to the movies with me tonight?"

"Yes, I would love to go to the movies with you, Derek. What are we going to see?"

Davey and Derek shared "TT" (twin telepathy).

What did you tell Abby, Davey?

I gave her a choice of two movies and she chose the super hero one.

Oh, good. I don't want to see a scary one with Holly. You know how I get when I scream. I sound like a girl!

Ha ha, I know!

"Derek, are you still there?"

"Oh, sorry, Holly. I was discussing the movie that we're going to see. I guess we'll see the super hero one if that is okay with you."

"Yeah, I love super hero movies! Great. What time are we going?"

What time did you tell Abby, Davey?

Oh, for goodness sake, Derek. Didn't you listen to anything I said?

No, I was too scared to listen. I was thinking about what I was going to say to Holly.

Davey sighed, *I told her that Dad will pick her up at 6:15 to give us time to buy concessions.*

Okay, sounds good to me, the more concessions we get the better. Derek guffawed.

"Derek, are you still there?"

"Yeah, sorry again. We were discussing times. We'll pick you both up at 6:15 for the 7:00 pm movies. Okay?"

"Okay, let me ask my mother if it's okay. Abby has to ask her mother too. Wait a minute."

Abby had already run out into the kitchen to see her mother about permission.

"Hey Mom, can I go with Davey to the movies tonight at 7:00?"

Holly put the phone down on the desk and rushed out to the kitchen to ask her mother the same thing.

"Mom, can I go with Derek to the movies tonight at 7:00? His father is coming to pick us up at 6:15 pm."

Jane and Shirley exchanged nods and said in unison, "Sure, but don't be home too late."

"Hurray, thanks, Mom!" Abby hugged her mother and raced back to the den.

"Thank you, Mom, too!" Holly squeezed her mother and kissed her cheek before running into the den and nearly knocking Abby over to grab the phone.

Abby stepped aside and handed the phone to Holly. "The answer is 'yes', Derek. Tell Davey too. We can't wait to go. See you at 6:15 pm."

Derek gulped and said, "Great. See you then."

He put down the phone and looked at his brother with a wide-eyed stare that said more than he could right now. He was speechless. It was going to be their first movie date with the girls.

Davey slapped his brother on the back and laughed. "Good for you, Derek! You did it! We're going to the movies for the first time with girls."

"Yeah, umm, I'm nervous, Davey."

"What are you nervous about?"

"I don't know. What do I say to her?"

"You don't say anything, silly goose. It's a movie and you don't have to talk. That's the beauty of a movie date. You both sit there and watch the movie and eat popcorn and junk and drink soda."

"Oh, I can do that! Wow, that's great. I don't have to talk at all and can eat all I want!"

"Yeah, I figured you'd like that, Derek," Davey hooted.

****

"Wow, we have a date, Holly! This is our second date with the twins."

"It's perfect because we can be together and we don't have to talk to the boys. We just watch the movie and eat. How great is that?"

"I figured you'd like that, Holly. I'm happy about it too. Maybe we can stop after and get an ice cream at Mini's."

"Oh, you and your ice cream, Abby!"

"Well, you and your popcorn and candy, Holly!"

Both girls giggled and swiftly took the stairs to their room to pick out outfits to wear later that night on their dates. They were unaware of being observed by two specters.

***

Minerva and Felicity were up at the ceiling taking in the excited faces and actions of the girls as they chattered away about their dates. The phantoms tried not to giggle to give themselves away.

But a warning sound suddenly disrupted their laughter. This sound was heard only by them and made them swiftly disappear through the cracks in the door panel into the passageways and out through the attic.

CHAPTER SIXTEEN

Warning from Mianna

Mianna was upset when she saw something in her crystal ball and called out to Felicity and Minerva to come quickly. Felicity could travel outside the house but Minerva couldn't without the help of Mianna.

Mianna sent a cloud for Minerva to ride on and follow close behind

Felicity to arrive at Gigi's house where Mianna (Gigi's cat's spirit) lived inside a crystal ball.

Gigi welcomed the ghosts into her room where she kept the crystal ball. Mianna's agitated face could be seen looking back at them. Gigi explained, "Mianna is quite upset over what she has seen about to happen or soon to happen. It involves an airplane and an unfortunate event."

Felicity voiced her concern first, *does this involve Holly's father by any chance?*

Yes, it does, Felicity. I'm sorry but I cannot control this event. I can only warn you about it. Maybe you can prepare Holly for the worst. I am still

*watching it as it will play out. I'm not
sure if he...*

What, Mianna? What is it? Minerva
sighed heavily and the sound of bees
were heard gathering around her.

*Mianna, please tell us what is
happening. Has it taken place yet?*
Felicity asked hesitantly.

*No, not yet but I can see it in the very
near future. There is a small plane
carrying six people, doctors, nurses
and other staff and equipment to an
island hospital.*

When will this happen, Mianna?

*I expect it will be in the next several
hours. I will keep watch and let you
know the outcome. I wanted you to be
close to Holly when she learns of this.*

Don't tell her that you know about it. It will get her upset too soon. Her father may survive it yet.

Oh my goodness, Felicity. What are we to do? Minerva cried without any tears or sound.

Minerva, please stay calm. If we get upset it will make the girls suspicious. We need to stay away from them. They are happy now. Let them be happy for a little longer.

Okay, Felicity, but I wish I could have a sound to voice my cries.

No, you mustn't have one. You will alert the girls and they will know something is wrong if they hear a sound from you.

Oh my goodness. I don't know what to do.

Relax, Minerva. It's time for us to leave. Thank you, Mianna and Gigi. We will keep an eye on Holly and wait until we hear from you about what has finally happened.

Heed my warning – do not tell Holly until I instruct you to tell her what I have seen.

Felicity and Minerva nodded and flew away. Felicity in the lead and Minerva close behind on her cloud.

As the ghosts got nearer to the old Victorian they saw a car coming up the street preparing to turn into the driveway. The ghosts ducked into the side of the yard so no one would see

them and floated up to the attic where
they found a spot to slip in.

Felicity and Minerva now safely back
at the foyer listened to the girls
talking to their mothers about going
on their first movie date with the
Donato twins.

*Oh, Felicity, I can't believe what is
going to happen to Holly's father.
What can we do to help Holly?*

*We need to keep her company
through the worst times, Minerva. We
need to stay calm. You need to stay
calm. You are making me nervous.*

*I'm so sorry, Felicity I can't help
feeling like this. I was always a
nervous child. I guess things don't
change when you're a ghost.* Bees

could be heard buzzing around as Minerva sighed heavily.

Shh, you must be quiet with all your sound effects, Minerva. Felicity controlled her human sigh in fear that the girls would hear them and look up. She put a cloak of silence around her and Minerva just in case.

Felicity thought over what they could do to help Holly through this unfortunate event. She only wished she had more powers to control the future. But she knew that even powerful Mianna was helpless to do anything to stop what was coming.

CHAPTER SEVENTEEN

Waiting for the Twins

The girls waited at the front window of the living room. They were too excited to even sit down on the couch. They kept looking out the window and sighing in anticipation.

Jane and Shirley sat on the couch and chatted and watched the girls nervously jump at every sound of cars coming up the street.

Finally, at 6:13 pm a car pulled into their driveway and two boys got out and walked up the path to the house.

The girls opened the door a second before Davey raised his hand to knock. The twins jumped in alarm when the door opened abruptly and two heads peeked out.

"Oh, sorry, Davey and Derek. We heard you coming up the drive," Abby announced eagerly, her cheeks flushed from excitement.

Jane leaned out the door and waved at the twins' father, Dan, in the car and asked the boys, "Do you want to come in?"

"Oh, no thank you, Mrs. Rizzo. We need to get going. There will be a long line to get our popcorn and stuff," Davey answered politely.

"Okay, but remember to get the girls home by 10:00 pm, right after the movies. Okay, boys?"

Shirley nodded at the boys, too, and introduced herself. "Hi Davey and Derek. It's nice to finally meet you. I am Holly's mother."

"Nice to meet you, Mrs. Lester," Derek responded. "We promise to get the girls home right after the movie. I think it's about two hours and fifteen minutes long."

"It could be close to ten or a little after with all the commercials and coming attractions, Mrs. Lester," Davey added.

"Okay, as long as it is right after the movie. I understand how long the movies are nowadays."

The girls hugged their mothers and said, "Thanks. We'll be home in time. Bye."

The foursome walked quickly to the car and the boys opened the doors for their dates and hopped in beside them.

They waved to Jane and Shirley as Dan Donato backed out of the drive and drove away.

Jane looked at Shirley when she heard sniffling. "Are you all right, Sis?"

"Yes, Jane. I'm so happy to be here to see my daughter go on her second date. I may have missed the first one but I won't miss any of the rest."

"Of course, you won't, Shirl. Our girls are growing up. Next month they will be twelve. (The girls' birthdays were only a week apart.) We should start thinking about what kind of party we can give them. They are such good girls and so helpful. If they hadn't done all their chores we would be scrubbing for hours more each day."

"Yeah, now we have plenty of time to relax and clean up the kitchen and finish the folding of the laundry," Shirley chuckled.

"Yep, it's nothing that we can't handle, Shirl. I'm so happy to have you here. I love you bunches!"

"Me too, Jane!" they chortled as they walked arm in arm to the kitchen and laundry to finish up their tasks with a smile.

They were unaware of impending doom which was soon to descend upon the Rizzo's and Lester's peaceful happy home.

CHAPTER EIGHTEEN

A Fun Night

The four preteens were excitedly chatting away about the super hero movie that they were going to see. In the front seat Dan Donato, a dutiful father, tried to block his ears of all the non-stop chatter.

He sighed in exasperation that he had gotten the duty to drive them to the movies over his wife. Laura Donato had told him that she would pick them up later that night so he could finish watching his coveted sports programs.

Dan couldn't wait to put his feet up, have a beer and pretzels and watch all the games that were coming on after eight. He pulled into the movie theater parking lot ten minutes later and announced, "We're here kids. All out that are getting out. Have a good time. Don't eat too much," he laughed knowing full well that his boys would eat plenty, especially Derek. He was just like him.

"Thanks Dad," the twins announced as usual in unison. This always surprised everyone who heard them speak together like that.

Abby also responded, "Thank you, Mr. Donato, for driving us tonight."

"Yes, thank you," Holly added.

"You are all welcome. Now, boys, listen, your mother will be here to pick you all up after the movie. I'll be busy."

"Okay, Dad, no problem. We know that you'll be watching your games," Davey chuckled.

"See ya later. Boys, have a good time and remember to be gentlemen at all times to the ladies."

"Yes, Dad. We know," Derek smirked and punched his brother's arm.

Davey rolled his eyes and waved at his father as he drove away. "Hey, are we ready to see some action, adventure and all that stuff?"

Everyone cheered and went into the theater to wait in line for their snacks.

The theater was full and the lines were long but at least moving a little. The four chatted comfortably now that they were getting to know one another better.

Abby whispered to Holly, "Should we tell the boys about the ghosts?"

"Hmm, maybe later. Let's get our popcorn and stuff then if we have time before the movie starts we can tell them."

Holly smiled and nodded. As the line moved she noticed some friends from school and called out to them and waved.

Abby did the same and smiled proudly that she and Holly had dates when the other girls did not. They were after all almost twelve now, nearly teenagers.

The foursome finally reached the counter, ordered their popcorn, candy, and drinks and headed into the theater. There were still ten minutes before the commercials and previews were to begin.

Davey led the way to the middle of the theater and found four seats that he thought were perfect. Davey wasn't so sure though.

Why did you choose these seats so far back? I like to be a little further down and on the end in case I have to get some more popcorn. I don't want to climb over tons of people.

Oh, Derek. Okay, move to your right and sit at the end.

Thanks, Davey. If you need anything I'll go get it for you.

Sure, whatever, Davey sighed.

"Where are we going, Davey?" Abby got up when she saw Derek moving further down the row.

"Oh, my brother wants to sit on the end in case he is starving for some more popcorn or whatever," Davey rolled his eyes and guffawed.

"Okay, sure. I don't mind sitting wherever you are," Abby rolled her eyes back at Davey.

"Oh, yeah. Okay," Davey's voice shook as he moved along quicker to claim a seat.

Holly exchanged questioning looks with Abby and sat down next to Derek as he handed her a drink and some candy.

"Thanks, Derek. I love red licorice, and peanuts and chocolate together. Can I have some popcorn too?"

"Oh, sorry. Help yourself."

Abby cleared her voice and tried to get Holly's attention. "Hey, Holly. I think we can tell the boys what we were talking about before. There is still time before the movie begins."

"Okay, you tell Davey and then he can tell Derek by 'TT.'"

Abby quickly relayed all that had happened with the ghosts' appearances. She watched the boys for their reactions as Davey told Derek in "TT."

Davey's face took on an animated expression and Derek's eyes opened wider with each new revelation. Finally he sighed and said, "Wow, I can't believe it! Now there are two of them. How cool is that?"

Holly smiled, "Yes, I agree, Derek. It is way cool. They are both so much fun to talk to and share stuff with. They have powers that are unbelievable too. Maybe you can come over and meet them sometime."

"Yeah, that would be awesome, huh, Davey?"

"Great, but now we have to be quiet. The movie is starting. Talk about this later. Okay?"

All nodded and gave the movie their rapt attention while they happily munched on their snacks and sipped drinks.

Two hours and thirty minutes later the kids headed outside to look for Laura Donato who was waiting close to the front door of the theater. She got out of the car and waved them over.

"Hey, how was the movie, kids?"

"Great, Mom. There was so much action and special effects my head is still spinning," Davey announced with flushed cheeks.

"It was fantastic, Mom! You and Dad should go see it sometime. You will love it too!"

"Yeah, if I can get your father off the couch and away from the TV. Happy to hear you enjoyed yourselves."

"I loved it too, Mrs. Donato," Abby reported when Laura looked her way.

"How about you, Holly? Did you like it?"

"Oh, yes, Mrs. Donato. I love all kinds of super heroes. They have unbelievable powers. I wish I could do some of that stuff."

"Well, I don't know if that would be a good thing, Holly, but nice to imagine anyway," Laura laughed

"Okay everyone, hop in. Boys, hold the doors for the girls please. Nicely done. Thank you," Laura smiled proudly at her boys.

"Thank you, Davey," Abby moved into the middle of the seat and Davey sat beside her.

"Thank you too, Derek." Abby scooted in to sit on the seat next to Holly.

Derek smiled and sat down next to Holly. He protectively held onto his leftover popcorn which he had gotten refilled earlier. It was going to be his snack when he got home if Davey didn't get to it first.

The four were quiet as they drove the short distance to the girls' house. They were all thinking about their discussion earlier of the ghosts.

"Okay, we're here, girls. Boys, walk them to their door."

"Sure, Mom," Davey and Derek chirped together.

The four whispered about the ghosts and made plans to get together another time when the boys could meet Felicity and Minerva.

"I'll check with our Mom about when we can come back here, okay?" Davey retorted.

"Yeah, we can say we want to see what your Dad has been doing in the house," Derek added.

"We noticed all the stuff in the bins outside. What's going on?" Derek queried.

"My father is making an apartment on the third floor for Holly and her family to live."

"Wow, that's great, Holly. Then you can stay here all the time with Abby," Derek exclaimed.

"Yeah, my mom is okay with that but my father is not. He's away now finishing up his time with Miracles Across Borders."

"Ok yeah, that's right. I remember you telling me that they were coming home and then your mother got sick. She's staying home though, right?" Derek waited for Holly to respond.

"Yeah, she's home for good and doing better."

"That's good!" Dcrck addcd with relief.

"Well, thank you, girls for coming with us today," Davey interjected.

"Yeah, thanks, Holly," Derek said shyly.

As the boys finished up their thanks, the door opened and Jane and Shirley stepped out to say 'hello' and wave at Laura in the car.

"We had a good time, boys. Thank you both," Abby and Holly added with a wave and went into the house.

Shirley and Jane waited for the girls to share their night with them as they sat down on the living room couch to finish drinking their coffees.

"Well, how was your first movie date, girls?"

"Great, Mom," Abby announced.

"Yeah, it was fun!" Holly responded.

The girls chatted on about the movie contents and how sweet the boys were to share their popcorn and candy.

They told their mothers what gentlemen the twins were to hold the door of the car for them to enter even before their mother suggested it.

"Nice to hear that they are such good boys," Jane said as she nodded to Shirley in relief.

"Well, it's getting late, girls. Head up and get ready for bed. So happy to hear that you had a good time," Jane said.

"Good night, girls. Sleep well. Love you bunches," Shirley proclaimed.

"Love you back, Mom!" Holly kissed her mother's cheek and then her aunt's.

Abby skipped over to them and did the same. "Good night, love you both."

Two specters flitted across the ceiling and flew through the secret passageways and up to the girls' room.

They wanted to be there when they were needed to give support. No word from Mianna yet but their senses were tingling and they knew any time now they would hear the news good or bad.

CHAPTER NINETEEN

An Unfortunate Event

The ghosts paced or more like flew back and forth across the ceiling of the girls' room. They were agitated and impatient. They had just returned from Mianna's with instructions about what to do next.

It was only 4:00 am and the girls were fast asleep. They didn't want to wake them up yet. But soon the whole household would be awakened by the news.

Jane sat up in bed and looked at the clock. The alarm hadn't gone off yet but she felt like something had awoken her. She didn't hear anything but it was more like she felt something strange. It was only 4:30 am and she usually woke up at 5:30 or 6:00 am. She didn't want to disturb Bob so she lie back down and tried to go to sleep again for at least another hour or so.

Up on the third floor Shirley was tossing and turning and having dreams that made her cry out. She sat up and looked at the clock. It was only 5:00 am. She was never a morning person. *What was that I was dreaming about? A plane and a fire and people screaming – what did that mean?*

Shirley rubbed her eyes and lie back down and fell asleep once again.

By 5:30 am Jane was up and raring to get the day started. She let her husband sleep a little longer until his alarm went off at 6:00 am. She quickly showered, dressed and went downstairs to start breakfast.

At 6:00 Bob was up and getting ready for work. As he usually did he turned on the television as he dressed to hear the latest news. What he heard and saw on the screen stopped him in his tracks. He grabbed his cell and called Jane down in the kitchen.

"Jane, turn on the television now. I'll be right down."

"What's going on, Bob? Did your team lose the game yesterday?" Jane laughed but heard only a dial tone as she reached for the TV remote.

Bob was out of breath as he came racing into the den and sat down next to Jane who was silent as she watched the screen in horror.

Jane reached for her husband's hand. "Oh, Bob, that's Jay's group, Miracles Across Borders. I pray he wasn't on that plane."

"Honey, don't jump to conclusions. There are many doctors, nurses and other staff flying back and forth all the time."

"I know, Bob, but we need to find out if he was. What about Shirley? Should we…"

"What about me?" Shirley stood behind Jane causing her to cry out.

"Oh my God, Shirley. I didn't want to wake you until we knew for certain that…"

"What, what's wrong, Jane. Tell me." Shirley's eyes went to the scene playing out on the television and dropped to her knees in horror. It was the dream she had earlier. Now it was happening in front of her.

"Oh, no, it can't be! I dreamt of this! I dreamt of this, dear God!"

"What did you say, Sis? How could you dream of this?"

"I...I don't know. I saw this happen in my dream. Is Jay dead? He can't be dead, please dear God!"

Jane put her arms around her sister and guided her to a chair. "I will call and find out, Shirl. Now don't worry. He's probably at another place right now."

"That's one of our planes. We took one like that before," Shirley's voice shook.

Bob grabbed the phone and called information to get a number for Miracles Across Borders. Jane got her sister a cup of coffee and sat next to her and hugged her to keep her from trembling. The women kept their eyes glued to the TV as the reporter described the carnage aboard the fiery crash. Ambulances and EMTs were at the scene as they tried to get closer while the flames were being extinguished by the fireman.

***

Upstairs on the second floor the girls were waking up and stretching and yawning. They both looked up in alarm as two ghosts appeared in front of them.

Abby and Holly could hear the ghosts' plea to wake and listen. They had something important to tell them.

"What's going on?" Abby looked at Holly and shrugged.

"I don't know. It sounds like Felicity and Minerva are upset about something. Let's listen."

Something has happened, Holly. You must go downstairs and be with your mother and family. They need you to be strong. Felicity waved her ghostly arm toward the stairs.

Go now, Holly and Abby. Go! Minerva stated as she flew up to the ceiling.

"What's wrong? Please tell me," Holly begged.

"What do you mean, Felicity? Please tell us," Abby beseeched as she grabbed some clothes and got dressed and pushed Holly to do the same.

We are here to give you support but you must be with your mother now. Felicity joined Minerva at the ceiling.

Holly ran downstairs with Abby right behind her. When they arrived in the kitchen they followed the sounds of the television in the den.

On the couch sat Jane and Shirley in each other's arms crying. The TV was displaying a fiery scene. Bob was on the phone and holding his head as he listened intently to the other end.

"Mom, what's wrong?" Holly stood over her mother and waited for her to look up and explain.

"Oh, Holly. I don't know yet what happened or how. Uncle Bob is going to tell us soon. I…"

"What? What are you talking about, Mom?" Holly sat next to her mother and took her hand that was cold as ice.

Jane spoke softly, "Holly, something terrible has happened. It involves the group that your mother and father are with, Miracles Across Borders. Uncle Bob is calling now to find out more information and whether your father was on the plane that crashed."

Abby held onto her cousin as she began to fall. Jane and Shirley rushed forward to catch Holly as she fainted.

"Abby, go get some water for Holly, quickly."

"Okay, Mom." Abby ran to the kitchen and came back with a glass of water. She held it up to Holly's lips as she came to.

"Are you okay, sweetheart?" Shirley gently touched her daughter's pale face.

"Oh, what happened?" Holly looked around at the shocked and stricken faces looking back at her.

"You fainted, honey," Jane stated.

"Is Dad okay? Was he on the plane, Mom?"

"We don't know yet, sweetie. We'll find out soon."

Bob put down the phone and sat on the couch next to Jane as the others settled on the second couch.

"What did you find out, Bob?" Jane asked gingerly.

"Well, there were several medical personnel on the plane. They are not sure who they are yet and how many may have survived the crash."

Shirley sniffled and gasped, "Oh dear God, please don't let it be Jay."

Holly sat next to her mother and hugged her tightly. "Mom, if I know Dad he will survive this. He is stronger than any of us."

"I know, sweetie, he is strong but…" Shirley stopped as she couldn't hold back her tears. She looked at her daughter and observed how very much she favored her father. This fact only made it harder to imagine that her husband could be gone forever.

"Bob, what did they say to you? Will they call you back and let us know for sure about Jay?"

"They were dealing with all the families concerned. As soon as they identify the passengers on the manifest they will call me to confirm if Jay is one of them."

"Okay, now we have to wait. Let's not get upset before we need to. It looks like some of the passengers did survive. Look at the ambulances racing off. If they were dead the ambulances wouldn't be taking the bodies but a hearse would instead."

"Yes, you're right, Jane. That's a positive thing. Thank you," Shirley sighed. "I know many of those people. We worked together for six months. We need to pray for the families of those who lost their lives, and for those who survived and that Jay survived too."

"Let's go into the kitchen. I was preparing breakfast. We all need to eat to keep up our strength for the news ahead. Sit down everyone while I finish the eggs and bacon. Girls, make the toast and set the table."

"Sure Mom."

"Okay, Aunt Jane."

Everyone mechanically ate breakfast and sat in a stupor with an ear toward the television as the newscaster kept saying the same things over and over again about the horrific scene.

CHAPTER TWENTY

News Arrives

Everyone stayed close to the television and phone all day waiting for some news of the survivors of the crash. The same scene played out on all the channels.

After lunch Bob tried calling the number for the medical group once again. He couldn't get through, waited some more, and tried again with the same result.

Close to dinner time the phone rang. Bob rushed to get it ahead of everyone else.

"Yes, this is Bob Rizzo. Are you sure? Yes, his name is Jay Lester. Okay. When will we know for sure? How long will that take? My family is anxious to hear. Okay. Please call me at this number. Thank you."

Bob sighed heavily and put the phone down. "Jay's name was on the manifest, but they can't find him anywhere. They're having trouble with matching up the passengers to the manifest. He is not the only one missing from the plane."

"What does that mean, Bob? How can that be?"

"Where is my Dad?" Holly cried out.

"Take it easy, honey. They're going to call me back when they know more. All the other families are waiting to hear too."

It was the longest night of their lives as they waited, certainly not with patience, for the phone to ring with news, hopefully good news.

Upstairs the ghosts chatted and sent good vibes back and forth trying to help the family as they waited.

Abby poked Holly and whispered, "Let's go upstairs and ask our ghostly friends what they know. Maybe they can help."

"Oh, I forgot all about them. They must have known about this. They woke us up, remember, Abby?"

"Yes, that's why I need to speak with them. Let's go upstairs."

"Hey, Mom. We're going upstairs to rest. Okay?"

"Sure, Abby. We'll call you if we hear anything at all."

"Thanks, Mom."

Felicity and Minerva waited at the ceiling and floated down as the girls came into their room.

"What can you tell us, Felicity?" Abby urged.

"Yes, you must know something," Holly pleaded.

We only know what Mianna told us this morning, that a plane had gone down in flames and could possibly have your father on board. We don't know anything more. As soon as we hear anything more from Mianna, we will tell you. I promise, Holly.

I'm so sorry, Holly. Minerva sighed as the sound of bees began to buzz around the room.

"Please tell me as soon as you hear anything, even if it's bad," Holly cried and threw herself onto the bed.

Abby lay next to Holly and patted her cousin's back. "It's going to be all right, Holly. Your father probably wasn't even on the plane. How else would it explain why they can't find him?"

"I don't know, Abby. All I know is that I couldn't go on if I lost my father."

"Oh, I know, Holly. I would feel the same if I…"

The ringing of the phone stopped Abby in mid-thought. The girls jumped off the bed and ran down the stairs taking two at a time.

Bob had once again picked up the phone and waved his hand to everyone to quiet down as he cried out in surprise, "Jay!"

Shirley and Holly rushed to grab the phone from Bob's hand but he handed it over to Shirley first.

Shirley's voice shook as she cried out, "Jay, are you all right? What…what happened?"

"I'm fine, honey. Don't worry, okay? I was fortunate not to be on the plane. At the last minute two of my patients took a turn for the worse so I didn't get to leave."

"Oh, thank God. But they reported you missing."

"Yes, that's because I was on the manifest and didn't call to cancel."

"Are you going to come home sooner now?"

"Honey, let's not talk about this now. We are all in shock over the loss of two of our staff plus the pilot and co-pilot. Four new staff members, two doctors and two nurses were badly burned and in critical condition. We need to pray that they will make it."

"Yes, you're right, Jay. I'm sorry. I won't pressure you. I'm just relieved that you're safe."

"Mom, can I talk to Dad, please?" Holly urged as she poked her on the arm.

"Honey, Holly wants to talk to you. Take care and call me again soon when you know more about the injured staff. Okay?"

Holly pulled the phone away from her mother before her father could say anything more. "Dad, I was so scared. Are you okay?"

"Yes, sweetie, I'm fine. Mom will explain what happened. You take care of your mother now. Okay? I will be calling again soon. Don't worry about anything."

"Okay, Dad. I love you."

"I love you too, sweetie. Bye for now."

"Bye, Dad."

Holly ran into her mother's open arms and cried tears of relief.

"It's over, sweetheart. Your dad's okay."

Jane and Bob circled Shirley and Holly in a protective hug.

THE END

A NOTE FROM THE AUTHOR

Watch for Book 3 coming in 2019!

Thank you for purchasing one of Jemsbooks. If you like this book, a review would be greatly appreciated wherever you purchased it. Word of mouth is the best way to spread word of books. Please share your review with friends and family. I would love to hear from you about my books.

Please go to my website for more children's books: http://www.jemsbooks.com.

All my books are available on Amazon and Barnes & Noble.

This is the second book in this middle-grade series. I plan to write a few more of these books in the next year or two.

In this book I touch on handling unexpected incidents and how to overcome disappointments in life.

The themes in all Jemsbooks deal in life lessons and teaching children how to be polite, kind, and sensitive to others' feelings. We need to remind children of all ages to treat one another with respect and kindness.

I want children to know that it's okay to be different. It is extremely important that all children feel safe and loved in their homes and in their lives.

I hope your children will enjoy these entertaining and fun stories and learn valuable lessons that will stay with them for a lifetime.

Look for more books in this series and the Davey & Derek series coming in 2018 and 2019, and a YA fantasy series coming in 2019 and 2020 and beyond.

With Blessings & Love,

Janice Spina

ABOUT THE AUTHOR

Janice Spina is a retired administrative secretary from a public school system in Massachusetts. She has always loved writing poetry and children's stories.

This is the second book in this middle-grade series. Janice has published eleven children's books for Preschool-Grade 3, five books in a middle-grade detective series for boys, one in the middle-grade Series for girls under Janice Spina and three novels and a short story collection under J.E. Spina. She continues to write more children's books and is in the process of editing more books for publication.

Janice's books have received twelve book Awards – one Mom's Choice Award, eight Pinnacle Book Achievement Awards, two from Reader's Favorite Book Awards – Honorable Mention and a Silver Medal, and a Silver Medal from Authorsdb Cover Contest and was a Finalist in Authorsdb First Lines Contest.

Janice loves to hear from readers and fans and will share your reviews on her blog if you contact her at jjspina@myfairpoint.net.

Look for more Jemsbooks on her website

http://www.jemsbooks.com

Amazon Author Page for all Jemsbooks:

http://amazon.com/author/janicespina7

Follow her on:

Twitter:

http://twitter.com/janice_spina

Facebook Main Page:

http://www.facebook.com/janice.spina.9

FB Author Page:

http//www.facebook.com/janicespina7

FB Novelist Page:

http://www.facebook.com/jespina77

She also has a blog:

http://www.jemsbooks.blog

Janice lives in New Hampshire with her husband, John, who is her illustrator/cover creator, and two aquariums of fish – one saltwater and the other fresh water.

Janice's slogan is: ***Reading Gives You Wings to Fly! Soar with Jemsbooks.com all year through!***

Happy reading! Reading is good for your health!

ABOUT THE ILLUSTRATOR

Dr. John Spina is a retired elementary and middle school principal from a public school system in Massachusetts. John has a doctorate in Educational Administration.

John has illustrated and created covers for eleven children's books for PS-Grade 3. This is the second book in this middle-grade series he has illustrated.

He has also created the covers for Janice's three novels, ***Hunting Mariah, How Far Is Heaven, Mariah's Revenge,*** and a short story collection, ***An Angel Among Us,*** all of which she wrote under J.E. Spina.

He is currently working on illustrating more of Janice's books and covers in between being the caretaker of their two tanks of fish.

Their joint goal is to encourage children of all ages to read.

Reading has been documented to be good for your health. Happy Reading!